I0531452

BOOK BITES

VOLUME 1

EXCERPTS FROM FOURTEEN BEST SELLING AND AWARD WINNING AUTHORS

Bonnie Edwards

Donna Fasano

Traci Hall

Dani Haviland

Mary Leo

Dorothy McFalls

Nancy Radke

Mona Risk

Jacquie Rogers

Jennifer St. Giles

Alicia Street

Helen Scott Taylor

Katy Walters

Patrice Wilton

Copyright

2015

by Chill Out!

No portion of this book may be reproduced without the author's written permission. All events, characters, names, and or places are fictitious or used in a fictitious manner and are used solely for entertainment purposes. Individual copyrights for each author's work also applies.

ISBN 978-0692465820

Authors' Billboard Introduction:

The Authors Billboard is proud to provide Book Bites 1 in print from.

This collection of excerpts from our group of authors will give you a taste of the wonderful stories we have available.

Please come and visit our website
http://www.authorsbillboard.com and meet our authors.
We run promotions on the second weekend every month with a fabulous selection of free and reduced priced books.

Sign up for our newsletter now and never miss a sale! Each month we'll pull the names of 10 lucky winners who get to choose a book from the sale page absolutely free.

Hope to see you over at Authors' Billboard
(**www.authorsbillboard.com**) soon!

Contents

VALENTINE BABIES

Holiday Babies Series

by

USA TODAY BEST SELLING AUTHOR

Mona Risk

Around the World with Stories that Simmer with Emotion.

Copyright © 2013 Mona Risk

Book Description

VALENTINE BABIES is a heartwarming story that will take you from the heart of Kentucky to South Florida and Atlanta, and then to Iraq and Germany.

Fearless reporter, Roxanne Ramsay, doesn't think twice before traveling for important assignments, even in a war zone—until her last trip leads her to a life-altering mistake.

At his best friends' wedding, Dr. Greg Hayes, who has a serious phobia of planes, can't take his eyes off the lovely maid of honor. But why is Roxanne blinking away tears? Getting involved with the strong-headed and too generous reporter involves more complications than the bright doctor has ever faced in the OR. Yet what wouldn't he do to save the love of his life and her baby?

Praise

"Mona Risk knows how to pull a reader into the minds of her well-crafted characters. Her work takes us on a journey be it local or overseas."

~Night Owl Reviews.

"Ms. Risk's writing sweeps you into the story and keeps you turning the pages."

~The Long and the Short of It Reviews

Chapter One

"Go now. And smile for heaven's sake," the wedding coordinator sputtered against Roxanne's ear. "It's your sister's happiest day."

The Mendelssohn Wedding March chimed through the Cathedral of Christ the King in Lexington, Kentucky.

Roxanne Ramsay plastered a wide smile on her face and clutched her poinsettia bouquet to stop the trembling of her hands. God only knew how happy she was for Madelyn and Nick.

But why did she have to receive that horrible email yesterday? Two days before Christmas. Last night, she'd claimed to suffer a twenty-four hour bug to avoid the church rehearsal and dinner. Honestly, she didn't have to fake stomach cramps. Her guts had twisted the moment she read and re-read the missive announcing Nabil's death. Alone in her room in the big empty house, she'd cried her heart out.

A new bout of tears invaded her eyes. She blinked furiously and shuffled forward. Had the aisle lengthened all of a sudden? Gliding on the white carpet, she thought she'd already covered a mile. Behind her, the four bridesmaids progressed at the same snail's pace.

Finally Roxanne reached the altar and sidled to the left. The fresh pine scent of the Christmas trees decorating the church mingled with the sweet fragrance of white roses in two vases adorning the altar. A delightful smell. Her stomach heaved.

Oh God, no. She braced herself and swallowed. The nausea passed.

Two of her sisters took the one-year-old flower girls Nick was holding in his arms and sat them next to their grandmother, and then the bridesmaids lined up beside Roxanne. They all

3

turned to watch the bride advance toward her groom.

The ushers and bridesmaids smiled as Nick took Madelyn's hand. Roxanne's face hurt from the effort of stretching her lips. In the first row, Mom sniffled and wiped her eyes with a lacy handkerchief. Could the sister of the bride cry as freely without attracting attention?

Why should she smile? There was no groom and no happy ending in her future.

When they all faced the altar, she allowed herself a few tears. Nabil's handsome face popped into her mind. Afraid she'd burst into a torrent of sobs, she bit hard on the inside of her cheek.

"Since when were you such a mushy one? You're crying even more than Mom," her sister Heather mumbled in her ear.

"Sorry. It's a... a special moment." She exhaled and almost hiccupped. *Please, God, help me stop crying.*

"Still people are wondering," Heather muttered in the same hushed tone.

"What people? We're facing the altar. Father O'Brien is too busy reading his holy words."

"The man standing next to Nick's dad's wheelchair hasn't stopped staring at you."

Roxanne's head spun to the right. That gorgeous groomsman in a black tux and neatly combed brown hair?

His hazel eyes captured her gaze. She hadn't attended last night's rehearsal and hadn't met Nick's friends. His frown relaxed and he smiled. She tried to avert her eyes, and then threw another glance in his direction. He winked.

Her nerves already a shambles, she burst out laughing and caught his silent chuckle.

The bridesmaids gasped. Even Madelyn threw her a stunned look.

"What is wrong with you?" Heather chastised.

"The rings, please," the priest said. He waited for an instant, surveyed the bridal party, and scowled at each of the ten members. None of them responded. "St. Anthony, help us. Who has the rings?"

The dashing groomsman was still staring at Roxanne and grinning.

"Greg?" Nick grunted. "Where are the rings?"

"Oh, sorry. Here." Greg extracted the rings from his pocket and handed them to the priest. Turning toward the bride and groom, Greg kept her in his line of vision, but assumed a more serious expression.

"You may kiss the bride." Father O'Brien exhaled and finished the ceremony

Roxanne lowered her head. *No more kisses for you. Never again.* A few tears escaped her.

Beside her, Heather hissed and handed her a tissue. Roxanne wiped her eyes and caught Greg's gaze. He wasn't smiling anymore. Astonishment puckered his forehead. He raised an eyebrow, silently questioning her. She turned to admire the newlyweds. Finally, Nick released his bride after an endless and nerve-racking kiss.

Time for congratulations. Roxanne inhaled, forced a weak smile, and threw her arms around Madelyn's neck. "Sweetie, I'm so happy for you." She sniffled again. "So happy," she mumbled between tears.

"Thank you, Roxy. And here I thought you were the cool-headed one among us. The unflappable globe-trotting reporter who runs around the world." Madelyn patted her cheek. "If you cry that much at a wedding, what will you do at a funeral, you softie?"

"Fu...funeral? Oh no." Roxanne swallowed a sob. She wouldn't even attend *his* funeral.

"Mrs. Preston, my darling, let's go." Nick grabbed his wife's arm. Hand in hand, they sauntered down the aisle toward the door of the church and waited to receive the guests' congratulations.

Thank God, it was over. The nightmare was over. *I mean*

the wedding.

"It's almost over. You can stop crying." Greg scooted next to her and arched a quizzical eyebrow. He pulled a tissue from his pocket and handed it to her.

"It was only a couple of tears." Carefully, she dabbed the wet spots on her face and raised her head for his evaluation. "I hope I don't look awful. My makeup?"

"Makeup is stable." He grinned widely. "You look lovely." He tucked her hand under his arm and they proceeded down the aisle. Behind them, the cortege of bridesmaids and ushers followed. "By the way, I am Greg Hayes. I work with Nick at St. Lucy's hospital, in Fort Lauderdale. And you are Roxanne, right? The sister who was sick last night."

He was doing his best to cheer her up. Nice guy. And so striking. Green specks twinkled in his hazel eyes. "Stomach bug." She patted her belly.

"Are you feeling better today?"

"Oh yes."

"So why were you crying so much?"

"Emotion. I'm so happy for my sister and Nick. " She sniffled and eased out of his hold, now that they'd reached the door.

A moment later, the coordinator called them for pictures. They regrouped in front of the altar.

"Bride and groom first." The photographer shot picture after picture. "Now the families. Bride and groom. His dad on his right." He checked the camera. "Great. Now the bride's family." They moved Roxanne next to her mother, first, then next to the bride. Her eyes focused on the camera, and then behind, on the second row where Greg sat, an ambiguous smile on his lips.

Darn, couldn't he stop watching her? When would this night be over?

~*~

Greg saw the two women in burgundy exit the restroom of the Marriott Hotel chosen for the wedding reception. He hesitated. The blonde one turned and held the brunette's shoulders. "Roxy, wait."

From the minute he'd seen Roxanne proceed along the aisle of the church, he hadn't stopped thinking of her, seeking her. Her exquisite face with greenish blue eyes, delicate features, and full lips had left an indelible imprint in his mind. He wanted to know her better. Maybe take her out.

"I've never seen you like that. Bad news? How can I help?" the blonde woman said.

Afraid to intrude, Greg backed up into a shadowy corner of the corridor.

"No one can, Tiffany. It's too late." The sadness of Roxanne's statement froze him in his tracks. He needed to know why this lovely young woman was suffering.

"At least, share with me."

"Tomorrow, I promise. We can't ruin Madelyn's wedding reception."

"No, we can't. Are you going to be able to say your toast?"

"Yes. If I cry, they'll think it's emotion."

The young women hugged each other.

Greg swore he would distract Roxanne. Maybe she'd forget her pain if she danced and chatted and laughed. He waited until they reached the hall and meandered toward her. "Here's my gorgeous date."

"Look, I'm in no mood for jokes." She strode toward the ladies room again and he rushed behind her.

"Roxanne, I'm sorry." He caught up with her. "Look, last night, your family told me what a fun adventurous girl you were. Tonight I saw a deeply distressed person. I just met you a moment ago, so I don't have the right to ask questions. For your sister and your family's sake, you can't afford to collapse. No matter what troubles you. Let me help and distract you."

She heaved a deep sigh. "I wish I could be distracted. But—

"

"Give yourself a chance to relax. Come let's have a drink. Soon they'll call our names and we'll make our entry into the reception hall."

Her gaze moved over his face and questioned. "Why do you want to help me?" Confused and weary, she frowned and blinked.

"Because I'm a doctor. I'm used to helping patients and people in need." He smiled. "And because I'm used to treating my dates well."

"Ah, do you often date?" She arched a curious eyebrow.

"I won't tell. But I can show you how you'll have a good time with me."

"Presumptuous man." She chuckled. Finally.

"Come on. The coordinator is lining up the bridal party. Let's not make her wait." He captured Roxanne's hand.

"The woman is already upset at me." Roxanne shrugged. "So are Heather and the photographer."

"Who cares?" They both burst out laughing. Greg loved the sound of her laughter. He wished he could restore her serenity and discover the young woman who wasn't afraid to travel to dangerous areas on difficult missions.

"Miss Roxanne Ramsay, the maid of honor and sister of the bride. And Dr. Greg Hayes, the groom's best friend." They strolled hand in hand to the dance floor and waited for the rest of the cortege to be called in.

"And now, the newly wedded, Dr. Nicolas Preston and Dr. Madelyn Preston."

The guests cheered. The bride and groom entered and the musicians played their favorite piece. They danced alone first, then couples joined them. "Shall we?" Greg asked.

She turned to face him. He smiled, pleased to have her in his arms. If everything went well, he hoped he'd keep her there a good part of the evening.

The song was a slow. Exactly what he needed. His chin

against her head, he held her tight and inhaled her floral perfume. A thorny and delicate rose.

When the music ended he walked her to their places at the bridal table. "Can I get you a drink?"

"Thanks, I'm good with my glass of water. We'll give the toasts soon."

Someone brought the microphone to Nick's father who delivered the first congratulatory speech, then it was Greg's turn. He stood and raised his champagne flute. "Nick, my friend, you sure are a lucky fellow. You've managed to get yourself a fantastic wife. You're my boss, so I think I should learn from you." The crowd laughed and applauded. "To the bride and groom, long life and happiness." Greg emptied his drink and glanced at Roxanne. She'd raised her flute but didn't bring it to her lips.

"My turn." She grabbed the microphone. "Maddy, you and I have shared a lot while growing up. You don't need my wise advice anymore." She chuckled. "I'm glad to let you go to a man who adores you and will make you happy. Nick, welcome to our family. You'll have to contend now with several attentive sisters-in-law and a mother-in-law who'll shower you with delicious cookies and good advice. To the bride and groom, long life and happiness."

Exuberant applause greeted Roxanne's toast. Everyone sipped their champagne. Roxanne abstained and sat her glass on the table.

Why wasn't she drinking champagne at her own sister's wedding? Even a sip? Instead, she nibbled on a French roll.

The waiters brought the salad, and later, the entrees. He and Roxanne chatted while eating.

"I heard you're well-traveled." Greg studied her curiously.

"I'm a reporter at KNR Television Network. So I'm always on the road or flying somewhere." Her whole face perked up at the mention of her work.

Pleased he got a positive reaction, he continued with the

same line of questions. "Have you ever interviewed a famous athlete?

"Quite a few," she said as if it were nothing extraordinary.

"Any presidents?"

"Not personally, but I was on the teams that met with French Pesident Sarkozy, South African Nelson Mandela, and the Prime Minister of India."

"Boy, you're an interesting person."

Her eyes sparkled at his compliment.

Finally he'd been granted a glimpse of the girl her whole family bragged about. "Any Royalty?"

"I had the incredible chance to talk to King Juan-Carlos of Spain when he was attending a special bullfight sponsored by the European Press."

"No kidding?"

"And the King of Sweden when he was a guest on the yacht of one of our famous billionaires. We exchanged a few words."

"Wow." He squinted, searching for more challenging questions. "Ever ridden on an elephant?"

She nodded. "Yes, in India and Thailand."

"How I wish I could have been there. How about a camel?"

She tilted her head and peered at him. "Are we playing a game? Know you in 10 questions or something like that? Because I'm good at questioning people too."

He burst out laughing. "Fine by me. I'll answer your ten questions when we're done with mine." At least, he'd managed to help her bury the disturbing thoughts that had plagued her at the church. "Can we continue?"

"Okay, I toured around the pyramids of Egypt on a camel."

"Lucky girl. To think I've never been north of New York. I never crossed any ocean. You must have so many stories to tell."

"Actually, I wrote about and reported on many historical events."

"Did you ever visit a war zone?"

Her smile disappeared. It was as if he'd lowered a shutter

10

over the brightness of her eyes. "Yes." She stared at her plate and forked her meat. Her lips pinched in a sad line.

Damn his question. He must have touched a raw nerve. Had she lost someone dear during a war?

"You don't like this question. Is it part of what disturbs you so much?"

"Yes." Her voice came as a hardly audible whisper.

Now he'd spoiled his previous effort. He cleaned his plate. "You've hardly eaten anything?"

"I'm not very hungry today."

"Stomach problems?"

"Just emotion." She reached for another bread roll and munched on it. He'd bet his old car that the emotion she claimed had nothing to do with her sister's wedding and was all about her personal problems.

"Let's dance." Pushing out her chair, she stood.

For an instant, Greg stared at her. Had she decided his distraction methods were effective? What a girl. "Good idea."

He followed her, admiring her back. The round hips swayed enticingly and sent a surge of heat to his groin. *Bad idea.*

He forced his gaze to move higher. To her elegant neck and the artistic twist of brown hair high on her head. He could imagine brushing feathery kisses along the creamy length of her throat. *Bad, bad idea.*

On the dance floor, Roxanne didn't wait for him and mingled with the dancers. He joined her and wrapped an arm around her waist, swung her to the strong beat of the music, spun her into his arms and out again. She laughed and followed his fast-paced lead as they moved to the music.

His gaze locked onto her eyes, assessing her mood. A smile lingered on her lips and her cheeks flushed a pink hue. Once again, her distress had faded, kicked away by the fun of the moment and her resolve to fight her inner pain. Hope fluttered in the air. Greg allowed himself a sigh of relief and enjoyed his partner's liveliness.

The music stopped and the coordinator announced that the bride would throw her bouquet. Roxanne spun. Her eyebrows gathered in a scowl and panic furrowed her face. She started toward the door, but four bridesmaids caught her after a few steps and dragged her back to the dance floor. Greg eased beside her. She needed support. What was entertaining for the others obviously upset her.

"Be a good sport. It's Madelyn's night," Heather scolded.

"You don't have to catch it," Tiffany advised.

"Are you ready?" Her bouquet in hand, Madelyn surveyed the dozen young women waiting, their arms raised high, and swiveled to face away from them.

Only Roxanne stood on the side, her mouth a stern line, her fingers clenched over her stomach.

"One. Two. Three," the groom called. His bride balanced her flowers over her head but didn't throw.

"Come on. Toss it," the young women shouted.

Madelyn laughed and hurled the bouquet to the side. It hit Roxanne squarely in the chest. She automatically closed her arms around it.

"Bingo. Roxanne got it." Laughing and squealing, the female crowd encircled the maid of honor.

Madelyn ran to her sister and hugged her.

"You did it on purpose. Why?" Roxanne glared at the roses in her hands.

"For a good omen. I want you to have the happiness I enjoy. You'll be the next bride, Roxy."

The color drained from Roxanne's face. "No, I won't. I'll never get married."

Poor girl. She was back to step one, with sorrow gnawing at her heart.

"And now," the coordinator announced, "the groom will remove the bride's garter and toss it to the eligible bachelors. The lucky winner will share a dance and a kiss with the bouquet winner."

"Oh no," Roxanne wailed.

"Yes, yes," the crowd chanted, unaware of the drama.

Greg squeezed her hand. "It won't happen. I promise."

He'd have to catch the garter to protect her from an unwanted kiss.

An unwanted kiss he was dying to give her.

A Note from the Author

If you enjoyed this first chapter from Valentine Babies (Holiday Babies Series Book 2) you can find the whole book and the Holiday Babies Series at Amazon. Please recommend and review the book. Email me at mona@monarisk.com

Check my website for more books. www.monarisk.com

About the Author

USA Today Bestselling Author, Mona Risk, received an Outstanding Achiever Award from Affaire de Coeur Magazine. Her name has often been posted on the Amazon.com 100 Most Popular Authors in Romance list. She's a two time winner of Best Contemporary Romance of the Year from Readers Favorite; a winner of Best Romance Novel of the Year from Preditors & Editors Readers Poll; and an EPIC Award finalist.

A tireless traveler, Mona Risk writes contemporary romance, medical romance, and romantic suspense novels, all simmering with emotion, sprinkled with a good dose of humor and set in the fascinating places she visited— or in Florida, her paradise on Earth.

Contact

Mona Risk can be found at:
http://www.amazon.com/Mona-Risk
www.monarisk.com
On Twitter: @MonaRiskS
Facebook: www.facebook.com/MonaRisk
Sign up for my newsletter:_http://mad.ly/signups/111038/join

Other books by Mona Risk

HOLIDAY BABIES SERIES: Books in this series can be read in order or as stand-alone reads.

1. **Christmas Babies**: A sweet and powerful Christmas Story.

2. **Valentine Babies**: Can he love a woman expecting another man's baby?

3. **Mother's Day Babies**: Never too late to find love and happiness.

4. **Wedding Surprise**: Is it the worst or best wedding surprise?

Christmas Papa: Who's my Papa, Mommy? (Coming soon)

Holiday Babies Series Box contains the first three books.

An Unusual Christmas: Running away from Christmas, she found her HEA at the end of the world.

Her Christmas Cruise: The would-be honeymoon cruise may still bring happiness.

DOCTOR'S ORDERS BOX SET: A box set of three bestselling books at Amazon.com

Books in this series can be read in order or as stand-alone reads.

Babies in the Bargain: "ER" and "Grey's Anatomy" in the NICU.

Right Name, Wrong Man: What's a girl to do when she whispers another man's name in her fiancé's arms?

No More Lies: A lie that brings a smile or a truth drawing tears?

THE ARMY DOCTOR'S WEDDING

The Army Doctor's Series

by

USA TODAY BEST SELLING AUTHOR

Helen Scott Taylor

Copyright © 2013 Helen Scott Taylor

Book Description

Major Cameron Knight thrives on the danger of front-line battlefield medicine. Throwing himself into saving the lives of injured servicemen keeps the demons from his past away. When he rescues charity worker, Alice Conway, and a tiny newborn baby, he longs for a second chance to do the right thing, even if it means marrying a woman he barely knows so they can take the orphan baby to England for surgery. The brave, beautiful young woman and the orphan baby steal his heart. He wants to make the marriage real, but he can never care for them as he longs to while he is stationed overseas away from home.

Praise

"Grab a Kleenex because you are going to need it! This is one no romance lover should miss!"

~Teresa Hughes

"If you love a gentle, emotional, family orientated, well written story, one that stays with you long after you have finished it, then I recommend you read any and all of this series."

~Amazon Customer

Chapter One

Alice Conway stumbled across the arid, rocky ground, a precious newborn baby clutched to her chest. The rattle of gunfire sounded behind her, each shot searing along her nerves. The three African women with her held their children in their arms, still running fast. Alice couldn't keep up with them for much longer. Her legs felt so weary, the muscles weak and aching, her feet sore.

She glanced over her shoulder as a rebel jeep crested the hill behind, about two hundred yards back. Pure terror streaked through her. Her little group of survivors was nowhere near the refugee camp yet. She would not get these women and children to safety in time. They would all be mown down in a hail of bullets like the rest of the villagers.

Her breath sawed in and out, so loud in her ears that it took her a few moments to notice the rhythmic beat of a helicopter approaching. She blinked away dust and sweat and realized there were two helicopters coming from the direction of the refugee camp. Were they friendly?

If they were government troops, they were likely to fire on the rebels and cut down the women and children in the crossfire. Neither side fighting over this war-torn country cared about the safety of civilians. If the vulnerable died they were just collateral damage, or worse still they were raped and murdered to spread terror. The charity Alice worked for did its best to help the women and children, but it was like trying to hold back a tide of hatred.

The smaller helicopter drew level. Alice's heart leaped with hope at the NATO logo on the side. The rebel jeeps sped up behind them, bullets thudding into the ground all around. NATO soldiers returned fire. The other helicopter hovered, preparing to land fifty yards ahead.

An almighty bang sounded behind. Heat and dirt blasted in all directions. Spatters of burning fuel showered the area, setting the small dry bushes on fire. One of the jeeps must have exploded. Alice ducked her head and hugged the tiny baby, running faster.

A stab of hot pain jabbed her calf. She stumbled, tried to right herself, but knew she was going down. She threw out an arm to save herself and angled her body to protect the baby.

~*~

Poised at the door of the Merlin helicopter, ready to jump out, Maj. Cameron Knight recoiled at the thunderous sound as a shell hit a rebel jeep. With a fiery flash and burst of black smoke it exploded. His gaze jumped back to the women and children. The three native women had cowered, huddling together. He couldn't tell if they were injured, but the blonde woman had gone down.

Cameron shifted his boots on the metal rim of the door, his gaze darting from the ground to the downed woman. His fingers flexed on the strap that held his medical kit on his back, eager to be down there.

"Wait, Major." The voice of the captain in charge of the unit shouted over the noise.

Cameron outranked him but as a doctor his rank was meaningless in combat situations. He was supposed to do what he was told. Nevertheless, he'd learned a long time ago that the British army cut doctors a lot of slack, and he took every inch he could get. He was here to offer front-line medical care, life-saving resuscitation, and damage-control treatment in combat situations. He did what needed to be done even if it was dangerous.

The second the chopper touched down, Cameron leaped out and dashed towards the casualty. She hadn't moved since she fell. If she'd taken a bullet she might be bleeding out. There was no time to waste. With a curse, the captain sent two soldiers out

20

to protect him.

Doctors weren't supposed to be in the line of fire but the fact Cameron didn't carry a gun was irrelevant. He needed to be out here where the wounded were.

He slid to his knees beside the woman, a gun discharging over his head. He tuned out the metallic rattle and concentrated on the patient.

She groaned as he gently rolled her over. Her eyelashes fluttered, revealing blue eyes. "The baby," she whispered, trying to move the arm she had fallen on. She winced in pain and Cameron realized she had a cloth-wrapped bundle inside her jacket. He pushed aside the fabric to reveal the head of a tiny newborn. The infant had a unilateral cleft lip. Something to be checked when they got back to base.

"Major Knight, there are more rebels coming. You need to get the woman in the helicopter," the captain shouted.

Gesturing his acknowledgment, he examined her quickly. Blood covered her lower leg, but it was only a flesh wound. With a bloodied nose and bruised cheek, she'd probably have a couple of black eyes—but it was her arm that worried him most. It lay at a strange angle, almost certainly broken in a couple of places.

The baby's vitals should be checked, but that would have to wait until they were in the helicopter. Not that he could do much for the child if it were distressed. He certainly wasn't a neonatologist, and he didn't have the equipment to treat a newborn.

He signaled to his combat medical technician, who ran over with a stretcher. They lifted the woman on and carried her back to the helicopter.

Cameron tried to take the tightly wrapped baby from her good arm, but she hung on. "No."

"I need to examine him. The baby will be safe. You can still see the little guy."

"Okay." She released the infant.

Cameron unfolded the bright red and yellow fabric from the

tiny body, noting the tied-off umbilical cord, which should be dealt with. Tension gripped him while he completed his visual check. The child had not sustained an injury. He released a breath and took the baby's temperature and pulse.

"He seems fine." Cameron settled the boy in a secure pouch beneath a seat. They weren't outfitted with transport cribs.

He turned his attention back to the woman. "I'm Major Knight, a doctor with the British army."

From the few words she'd spoken he thought she had a British accent, but he wasn't certain. He recognized the logo on her jacket, a hand cradling a baby. It was a charity caring for women and children in conflict zones. "What's your name?" he asked gently as the helicopter rose into the air.

"Alice Conway. How are the others?" Raising her head, she tried to see. Cameron glanced over his shoulder to where the medical technician was checking the African women. They squatted in a group, their children tight to their sides. Their suspicious dark eyes fixed on the soldiers distrustfully. It was little wonder considering the way they were used to being treated.

Cameron pressed his lips together with a burst of frustration over how powerless the British army was to really make a difference here. As soon as NATO pulled out, everything would go back to how it was before. But now wasn't the time to say such a thing. He returned his attention to Alice and forced a smile. "They're safe." For now.

Alice relaxed and her eyelids fluttered as she fought to stay awake. "My arm hurts."

"I'm afraid it's broken, but we'll fix you up at the military field hospital."

"My leg burns as well."

"That's nothing to worry about. Just a flesh wound. I'll dress it in a moment. Let's make your arm more comfortable first."

The baby let out a thin, urgent wail. Alice reached out her good arm and touched the tiny bundle. "It's all right, sweetheart.

I'm here."

Whether the baby responded to her or it was just coincidence, Cameron didn't know, but the child quieted.

"He must be hungry," Alice said. "He was born about three hours ago and he hasn't been fed yet. I gave him a few drops of water on my finger but that's all I could do." A sigh whispered between her lips and her eyelids fell.

"I'll have him checked over by someone with more experience in pediatrics when we get to the hospital." Cameron stroked the sweaty blonde bangs off her forehead. He had an overwhelming urge to touch her, comfort her.

She shifted her position and a moan slipped between her lips.

"Your arm?"

"Yep."

"I'll give you a shot for the pain and strap it up."

~*~

It was so good to be safe, to be lying down with someone taking care of her. The doctor cut away the sleeve of her jacket to expose her arm. He retrieved a small glass ampoule from his pack and held it upside down before jabbing the syringe needle in and drawing out the liquid.

She closed her eyes as he gave her the shot, willing it to take effect. Her arm ached like crazy. Every time she moved, pain shot into her shoulder and down her body. The throb in her head and sting of her lower leg were nothing in comparison.

"We'll give that a few minutes to take effect before we move your arm."

Alice opened her eyes to find the doctor leaning over her. His fingers gently probed the bridge of her nose and beneath her eye.

His eyes were dark brown and gentle. A man who did his job must be kind and compassionate. His gaze moved to hers. A smile curved his lips and crinkled the corners of his eyes. "The good news is there're no bones broken in your face. You'll look like you've gone ten rounds with Mike Tyson, though."

She smiled in response, despite her pain. "What did you say your name was?"

"Major Knight." He leaned a little closer. "As you're a civilian, you can call me Cameron if you like."

Alice reached a hand towards the baby again and stroked the little cloth-wrapped bundle, hoping her touch let the tiny boy know he was safe. Just the thought of what the villagers would have done with him made her eyes tear up. All because the poor little guy had a cleft lip.

Cameron moved to work on her leg. Alice closed her eyes and drifted. She was so exhausted; she struggled to stay awake. She and the women from the village had run for three hours, driven by fear to reach the refugee camp on the outskirts of Rejerrah before the rebels found them.

The sound of the soldiers' voices merged with the noise of the helicopter engine and the floor vibrated against her back. Strange smells assailed her: the metallic stink of oil, the tang of antiseptic. Something cold rubbed over her leg. It stung, then paper ripped and a soft dressing pressed onto the wound.

Cameron touched her shoulder. "Are you okay, Alice?"

"Just dopey."

"Nothing to worry about. The analgesic has a mild sedative effect. Your leg wound is only minor. I suspect a stone or piece of debris hit you when the jeep exploded."

He pulled a blue sling out of his pack and unfolded the straps. "This is going to hurt a little, but your arm will be more comfortable once we have it supported."

Alice gritted her teeth against the jab of pain as Cameron gently moved her arm, folding the forearm against her chest before securing it in the sling. After fastening it, he touched a hand to her cheek. "There you go. That will keep it still until we reach the field hospital and set it properly."

"Will you do that?"

"I can if you like."

24

"Yes, please."

Alice didn't like men much. She'd seen enough evidence that they weren't to be trusted. Not just here, in the conflict zone, but back in Britain as well. Yet she did trust Cameron. There was something about him that made her feel safe. Maybe the red cross on his jacket sleeve, or maybe his caring smile, or the way he handled her so gently.

~*~

The tension eased from Cameron's shoulders. It looked like there was nothing seriously wrong with Alice. In a few weeks the minor injuries would have healed. By six weeks the broken arm would be mended as well.

Lifting the tiny baby, he settled him in the crook of Alice's good arm. Despite the ordeal the infant had suffered in its first few hours of life, its pulse was strong and its temperature normal. Some people were survivors and this baby seemed to be one of them.

With a smile, she kissed the baby's head. "You're such a good boy, aren't you, sweetie?"

She seemed very attached to the child considering he was only a few hours old and obviously not hers. How had she come to have him? From what he'd seen, she had fallen hard because she tried to protect the baby. That was why she'd hurt her arm. She'd protected the child at her own expense.

He glanced at the small blonde woman with respect. He did his bit to help the locals if they were sick or injured but he operated under the protection of the military. Charity workers like Alice had no such protection. Their charity status did not always shield them from violence.

"The baby's cleft lip can be repaired, can't it?" she asked, a note of concern in her voice.

Cameron poked his little finger in the child's mouth and explored the soft palate. "I can't feel a gap in the roof of the mouth. If it's only the lip involved, then the surgery is straightforward. You will need a plastic surgeon for it, though."

"ETA five minutes, Major," the captain said.

"Understood."

He fastened straps around Alice to secure her. "Hold the baby tight. We'll take you both in together on the stretcher."

"Where are we landing?" she asked.

"The military base at Rejerrah. You and this little guy will be admitted to the field hospital. I'm afraid the three women and their children will have to go to the refugee camp. At least they will have food and shelter and a measure of protection."

"As long as they're safe." Alice hugged the tiny boy and settled back on the stretcher as the helicopter landed.

The medical technician took one end of the stretcher and another soldier on the team took the other.

"Ready," Cameron said, touching the back of Alice's uninjured hand.

"Yes. I want to get myself sorted out quickly so I can look after the baby." She gripped Cameron's hand, and he met her determined blue gaze. "You will help me get the best care for him, won't you?"

"Of course."

"Promise?"

Cameron was taken aback. Patients didn't usually question his dedication to the job. Yet he could understand her being concerned for the baby.

"I promise I'll do whatever I can to ensure the little guy gets top-notch treatment."

A Note from the Author

If you enjoyed this chapter from *The Army Doctor's Wedding*, you can find the rest of the book and the other books in the Army Doctor's series at all main online retailers.

About the Author

USA Today bestselling author Helen Scott Taylor won the American Title IV contest in 2008. Her winning book, *The Magic Knot*, was published in 2009 to critical acclaim, received a starred review from *Booklist*, and was a *Booklist* top-ten romance for 2009. Since then she has published other novels, novellas, and short stories in both the UK and USA.

Sign up for Helen's newsletter here:
http://helenscotttaylor.us9.list-manage.com/subscribe?u=0eff300f4f4bab5097a48023f&id=cf59b54c26

Contact

Find Helen Scott Taylor at:
www.HelenScottTaylor.com
www.twitter.com/helenscotttaylo
www.facebook.com/helenscotttaylor
www.facebook.com/HelenScottTaylorAuthor

Other books by Helen Scott Taylor

The Army Doctor's Series. (Books can be read in order or as stand-alone reads.)

Prequel The Army Doctor's Forever Baby. Can their love survive a heartbreaking test?

#1 The Army Doctor's Baby. He falls in love with his brother's girlfriend

#2 The Army Doctor's Wedding. A marriage of convenience to adopt an orphan baby.

#3 The Army Doctor's Christmas Baby. Heartwarming Christmas romance.

#4 The Army Doctor's New Year's Baby. His commanding officer's sister is irresistible.

#5 The Army Doctor's Valentine's Baby. An abandoned baby brings two lonely doctors together.

#6 The Army Doctor's Honeymoon Baby. Best friends become lovers, but a family secret threatens their happiness.

Sweet Italian Christmas Trilogy

#1 Italian Christmas Proposal. Take a Christmas vacation in Italy and fall in love!

#2 Italian Christmas Baby. Emily has everything ready for the birth of her baby--the only thing left to do is tell the father!

#3 Italian Christmas Wedding. She runs from the Mafia straight into his arms!

Check Helen's website for other titles.
www.HelenScottTaylor.com

CATERED AFFAIR

by

USA TODAY BEST SELLING AUTHOR

Patrice Wilton

Copyright © 2014 Patrice Wilton

Book Description

A family tragedy has career-minded Jenna Cassali housebound with two teenagers, a baby, and a dog from hell, with a hot doctor in pursuit. The longer she stays the more she realizes what's missing in her own life, but she likes to play it safe, and safe means returning to New York and her job, not launching a catering business, or falling in love.

Grant, a pediatrician and widower, believes his son died because of his negligence. The hospital becomes his life, but when he meets Jenna, his broken heart begins to heal. Can he close the door on his past, and allow himself to love again? Will Jenna find the courage to change her destiny, open her life, and her heart?

Praise

"It was a delightfully complex book with a full range of emotions and a fully fleshed story"

~Guilty Pleasures Book Reviews.

"Characters were lovable and story was one that made me laugh and cry."

~KLDB

Chapter One

Jenna Cassali had a death grip on the steering wheel of the monster vehicle she drove, and a murderous glint in her eye. She'd like to wring her sister's neck right now.

Cindy had to be the most inconsiderate... No forget that, the most *reckless* person in the world. She had her five-month-old baby in the backseat of her car, but raced down I-95 like it was the Daytona speedway, with no regard for anyone's safety.

For the past several miles, Jenna tried to keep up, but she wasn't used to driving ten-ton gas-guzzlers in heavy traffic. As a New Yorker, she took cabs everywhere. She'd only arrived in Palm Beach yesterday for a three day visit.

This morning her sister had to take her new sexy red Mercedes convertible to the dealership for its five thousand mile inspection. Jenna had asked to drive the smaller, sportier vehicle, but then Cindy had decided she didn't want to waste time putting the baby-seat in the SUV, so Jenna got stuck driving the beast.

A familiar ring caught her attention. *Oh no.* She looked down at the cell phone on the passenger seat, knowing she'd have to answer. She relinquished one hand from the wheel, picked up the phone, and spoke. "Yes?"

"Hey, sis. You're lagging behind. If you can't keep up, remember we're getting off on Okeechobee. It's the next exit."

"So, why aren't you in the right lane? Slow down, will you?"

She'd always had suspicions about her sister, but now she knew Cindy was certifiably nuts. For the past several miles she'd watched her weaving in and out of traffic, dashing around huge trucks, driving at least ten miles over the speed limit.

"I'm living life in the fast lane," Cindy laughed.

"Not funny, moron."

"You need to put your big girl panties on, and have some fun. You're driving a tank, for heavens sake. Live a little."

If this was living, Cindy could have it. It was all Jenna could do to keep the SUV in the center of her lane while keeping an eye on her sister's car.

A mile back, Jenna had seen a warning sign that construction was ahead. She could see the traffic slowing, and also that Cindy had pulled out to pass another truck.

What was she doing? Jenna thought. Didn't she see cars braking ahead of her, slowing down to a stop?

"Cindy! Watch out. The cars are...."

The brake lights on Cindy's convertible suddenly flashed, and the car went into a skid. Jenna watched in horror as her sister's vehicle smashed into a truck, stopped in the left lane. The car immediately behind her had to swerve onto the shoulder to avoid a rear-end collision.

"Cindy! Cindy!" There was no answer.

Tears blurred her Jenna's vision as she slammed on her own breaks. All around her vehicles stopped. People raced to the scene of the accident. Jenna sat trembling, more scared than she'd ever been in her life.

She no longer wanted to kill her sister—she wanted to see her miraculously walk away from that smashed vehicle, thumbing her nose at death.

Jenna still had her cell phone in hand and punched in 911. When the dispatcher answered, she reported the accident and their location on 95. She then ran for Cindy's car. As she drew near enough to see the damage, she stopped and clutched her stomach. She felt as though she'd been hit by a cannonball.

She was light-headed, dizzy and nauseous. Cindy was dead. She had to be. Nobody could survive that. The front of the car was crumpled like an accordion.

Jenna lurched toward the wreck, but strong hands held her back. "That's my sister," she cried, trying to twist free. "Let me go. Please, let me go."

A big man stepped in front of her. "You should wait for the ambulance. It looks bad, miss. You don't want to see your sister right now."

She pushed past him and saw Cindy's head against the driver's window. The shattered glass was covered in blood. Cindy looked like a broken doll, her head twisted at an odd angle.

A moan escaped Jenna's lips, and her knees gave way. As she started to sink to the ground, the big man grabbed her and held her up.

"She has a baby in the back," Jenna choked out. "Please...let me see the baby."

"It's okay, miss. The baby looks fine."

In the distance she heard the wail of a siren. Looking around at the stalled vehicles in every lane of the highway, she wondered how long it would take them to get there. How long before Cindy would get help?

Rob! She pulled out her cell and punched in her sister's husband's number. She sobbed the second she heard his voice.

"Jenna? Is that you? Is something wrong?"

"Yes. Yes, Rob." She sucked in a breath. "I'm so sorry, but there's been an accident."

"Tell me." His voice was gruff. "Who's hurt?"

"Cindy," she whispered. "And Amy was with her."

As the sound of sirens got louder, she looked around to see an ambulance driving on the shoulder to get around the stalled traffic. A fire department rescue truck followed. The vehicles stopped, sirens still blaring. Paramedics and firefighters rushed to Cindy's car.

Jenna stayed on the phone with Rob, reporting what she was seeing.

"They've got Amy out and I can hear her crying. But they can't get Cindy's door open." Her nails dug into the palms of her hands. "Rob, I'm so scared."

"I know you are." His voice seemed unusually calm but she knew he must be freaking inside. "Focus on Amy for now. Where is she?" he asked. "How is she?"

33

Jenna ran over to the ambulance where one of the paramedics was checking Amy over. The medic told her the child was conscious and didn't have any apparent life-threatening injuries, but that she'd be transported to St. Mary's hospital for observation.

She passed on the information to Rob, and stayed on the phone, giving an account of the rescue team's actions.

A giant cutter that resembled scissors sliced through the roof of the car, snapping the car-door post like a twig. Powerful pincers inserted into the side of the vehicle pulled a section out. The machines tore the car apart as easily as if it were a can of sardines. But sardines weren't inside. It was her sister.

When the firefighters eased Cindy's body from the wrecked car and onto a stretcher, Jenna nearly whimpered. Cindy looked lifeless.

She stepped up to one of the firefighters. "Please…that's my sister…is she alive?"

"Yes. There's a pulse."

"Thank you." She spoke into her phone. "Did you hear that, Rob? She's alive, but unconscious. I'll see you at the hospital."

~*~

Jenna had no recollection of the drive, but she arrived a few minutes after her sister and niece were both wheeled into emergency.

"Are you her mother or next of kin?" the admitting nurse in the children's ward asked. "We need some paperwork filled out."

"Yes, I'm her aunt. Her mother was in the car with her and brought in separately."

The nurse handed her a clipboard of papers and told her to fill them out the best she could. Still feeling shell-shocked, Jenna headed to the waiting room, a bright, happy room, with plenty of toys and children in mind.

34

She forced herself to focus on the paperwork, but she didn't have any of her sister's insurance information. Still, Amy wouldn't simply be Baby Jane Doe. Jenna returned the mostly blank forms and went back to the waiting room. She didn't know how long she sat there, staring blankly at the brightly colored walls.

"Ms. Madison?"

She looked up. A tall man wearing a white lab coat stood in front of her. He looked to be in his mid-forties, with dark hair that was slightly graying, and deep creases around his mouth. She wondered if they came from smiling or the stress of the job. She figured the latter.

She stood, but her knees were wobbling so badly she didn't know if they'd keep her up. "I'm Jenna Cassali, Amy Madison's aunt."

"I'm Dr. Marshall." He shook her hand. "Are Amy's parents here?"

"Her mother was in the car with her, but..." She spotted Rob coming down the hall, and breathed a sigh of relief. "Here comes the father."

"Is Amy okay?" Rob asked when he reached them. His chest heaved as though he'd sprinted from the parking lot.

The doctor answered. "Amy is fine," he assured them. "She's resting right now. We'll need permission to keep her overnight."

"Keep her?" Rob's raised voice showed his strain. "Can't I take her home?"

"No, I'm afraid not." The doctor spoke gently as if to relieve their fears. "She needs to be observed."

"But you said nothing was wrong." Rob spoke harshly, and Jenna knew he was sick with worry.

"Rob?" She put her hand on his arm. "The doctor knows what's best for her. What's happening with Cindy?"

"It'll be hours before we hear anything. All I've been told is she has a head injury."

"Would you like to see Amy?" Dr. Marshall asked. "She has some bruises where the straps from her car seat held her, but no other apparent injuries."

They followed the doctor down the hall to Amy's room. Jenna wondered how he could do this sort of thing every day and apparently stay so calm and uninvolved. *Must have ice in his veins*, she decided.

He led them to Amy's crib. She was sleeping, and the doctor rubbed the baby's cheek with the back of his fingers, smiling down at her.

Rob's voice shook as he looked down at his daughter. "You're sure she's okay? She's going to wake up, isn't she?" He swiped at a tear. "I couldn't bear it if anything happened to her."

Jenna swallowed a big lump in her throat as she looked at Rob and the baby. He loved her so much. She had been an unexpected gift to the family. They already had two teenagers, and Cindy had thought her child-raising days were over until Amy came along.

"She's going to be just fine," the doctor answered. "I won't let anything happen to her, I promise." His genuine smile instilled trust.

There was no ice in this man's veins.

Jenna said softly, "Thank you for taking care of her." She ran a hand over Amy's back, remembering how her little body had felt in her arms just an hour earlier. "I know she's in good hands."

The doctor's gaze met hers over the crib, and she thought irrationally that his eyes were like melted honey.

He said, "I love the babies. But I'm happiest when I see them leave."

She smiled. "We'll be back in a little while. What time are the visiting hours over?"

"Come anytime. I'll leave word with the nurses to expect you regardless of the hour."

Rob reached out to shake his hand. "We appreciate that.

Thank you." After a last kiss for Amy, her brother-in-law followed Jenna into the hall.

"Let's go see how her mother is." Rob's expression was grim. It was obvious to Jenna that he feared the worst.

"She's going to make it, Rob. I know Cindy. It'll take more than this to keep her down."

His attempt at a smile came out as a twisted curl of his lips. The sorry effort tore at her heart.

They didn't say another word, but simply retraced their steps to the main wing of the hospital. When they reached the ER waiting room, Jenna said she'd go find some coffee and sandwiches.

"I can't eat." He looked at her with the saddest eyes she'd ever seen on a man. "I guess I need to call your mother. And mine." He ran a hand over his face, and his shoulders shook. A second or two later, he whispered, "How am I going to tell the kids?"

"You'll know what to say," Jenna said, and put a hand on his arm. "Do you want me to go get them?"

"Nick has his car. I'll call the school and have the kids meet us here."

"Yes, that's good." She stood, looking down at him for a moment. "Make the phone calls. I'll get the coffee."

She walked down the hall and got them each a cup of caffeine from a dispenser, and then returned to sit by his side. He had his long legs spread out in front of him and was staring at his feet.

"Here, Rob. I didn't know if you took it loaded or black, so I added cream and sugar."

He lifted his eyes to look at her. "Thanks." He sipped the steaming liquid, but she was pretty sure he didn't taste a thing. "Did you see her, Jenna? Was she cut up bad?"

"I saw her, but not up close. There was some blood, but at least her head didn't go through the windshield. The seatbelt and airbags protected her. She was unconscious."

37

Jenna tilted her head back and closed her eyes. Cindy had survived more than one catastrophe, and she would survive another. *Was there ever a time*, she wondered, *when Cindy hadn't walked the edge of disaster, with Jenna there to save her?*

"Did Cindy ever tell you about the time we got stung by bees?"

Rob shook his head, still staring at the floor.

"She was about six, and even then she was fearless. We had a rope swing tied to a tree, and Mom told us not to play on it because the bees had build a hive near the swing."

Jenna shook her head, and smiled at the memory. "You know Cindy. She didn't pay Mom any mind--or the bees either-- and got up on that rope. The bees buzzed around her as she swung, and she'd swat at them, but for some reason they left her alone."

Jenna couldn't tell if Rob was listening or not, but she continued with the story. "Eventually Cindy got tired of having to deal with them, and before I could stop her, she picked up a stick and hit the hive. Well, that was it! She'd pissed them off good, and now the bees swarmed out and attacked."

"What happened?" Rob asked.

"Cindy dropped to the ground, rolling around and screaming. The damned bees were all over her. I jumped in, and then Mom came running. She fought the bees off with a kitchen towel, grabbed us both and got us inside."

"I can't believe she never mentioned it."

"Maybe she forgot about it, but I never did." She drew in a shaky breath and continued, "We were both hospitalized, but Cindy had so many stings, the doctors thought she might die. I got blamed for allowing her to get too close to the hive."

"That was hardly fair."

"I didn't care." Jenna shrugged. "I just wanted her well."

When Cindy was lying in that hospital bed, her face swollen so bad that she couldn't open her eyes, Jenna had prayed to God, promising if He spared Cindy's life, she'd take better care of her.

She'd had lots of opportunities to make good on that promise when Cindy was in her teens. Jenna hadn't regretted a single one of them. *Hell, if I live to be a hundred, taking care of my sister will always be a priority.*

And more than anything, she wanted to be in the room with her right now, holding her hand and whispering encouragement in her ear--to let Cindy know that she was not alone and never would be.

Time passed slowly. After a long silence, Rob gave voice to his fears.

"If she has a head injury, it could take months for her to get better--could be as long as a year. I had a chef once whose wife had a brain injury after she drove into a pole. She was hospitalized for almost a year. Then she had to go through months of rehab."

He dropped his head in his hands and drew in a shaky breath. "I don't care how long it takes," he said, his voice rough with unshed tears. "I just want her back."

Jenna touched his arm. "Rob, we don't know anything yet. As far as we know, she might already be awake and talking."

He lifted his head to glare at her. "They would have shared the good news, don't you think?" His tone was bitter, but she didn't take offense. They were both worried sick.

Eventually a doctor walked toward them. "Are you Cindy Madison's next of kin?"

Rob stood up. "I'm her husband, and this is her sister. How is she?"

The doctor looked at them both. Jenna noticed his dark eyes were warm and steady. She relaxed a little.

"She's stabilized," he said in a deep baritone. "We had to insert a cerebral shunt to reduce the swelling. All we can do now is watch and wait."

"Is she awake?" Rob asked.

"No. I'm sorry," the doctor replied. "She's in a coma."

A Note from the Author

If you enjoyed this first chapter from Catered Affair you can find the whole book at:
http://amzn.com/B00K1MN1YO Please recommend and review the book.

About the Author

Patrice Wilton is a USA Today best selling author of more than twenty books, including her successful romantic comedy, **Candy Bar** series, and **Serendipity Falls** series, and returning war heroes, published by Amazon Montlake. When she's not writing, you might find her on the tennis court, or hitting golf balls with her PGA pro husband.

Contact

If you'd like to sign up for Patrice Wilton's newsletter to receive new release information, please visit **www.patricewilton.com**
Email me at **patricewilt@yahoo.com**
Follow on **Facebook**
https://www.facebook.com/patrice.wilton
and Twitter **@patricewilton**
Book updates can be found at **www.patricewilton.com**
http://www.amazon.com/Patrice-Wilton/e/B005MRS0KI/

Other Books by Patrice Wilton

Replacing Barnie – book one in the Candy Bar series
Where Wishes Come True – book two in the Candy Bar series
Night Music –book 3 in the Candy Bar series
For The Love Of Candy –book 4 in the Candy Bar series
A Hero Lies Within –Contemporary Romance
Handle With Care –Contemporary Romance
At First Sight—Contemporary Romance
Serendipity Falls – Romantic-comedy-book one in the
Serendipity Falls series.
Wedding Fever – Romantic-comedy- book two in the
Serendipity Falls series.
Love Struck – Romantic-comedy- book three in the
SERENDIPITY FALLS series.

A LADY'S PLIGHT

(Lord of Sussex Series Book 1)

by
Katy Walters

Copyright © 2014 Katy Walters

Book Description

Sweet and Spicy Historical Romance.

Lady Isabella Winton waited four years to marry her fiancé, but each year Lord Alexander Fitzroy, Earl of Standford, a serving officer and a reformed rake, finds an excuse to delay the nuptials. This time, with the marriage set for the next month, he tells her he received an urgent message from his Colonel. He is needed in Belgium almost immediately. He warns her it may be dangerous for her to accompany him.

Isabella realizes he is bluffing, things would not change so suddenly. Despite Napoleon's escape from Elba, Brussels is the centre of a social whirl. She looked forward to riding in the famous park off the Rue Royale; elaborate dinners and extravagant balls; so different from the quiet life in rural Sussex. Fearing Alex may have returned to his rakish ways and already installed a mistress, she insists on travelling with him.

Caught up in arrangements for a hurried wedding, Isabella is unaware Lord Everard Ladness, heir to a dukedom, is obsessed with her and will go to any lengths to possess her.

Praise:

"A wonderful picture of the times with a protagonist who evokes the qualities of independent females in the modern era."

~ZM

"I enjoy historical fiction and thoroughly enjoyed this one! It was a fun story and I look forward to the next in the series."

~LeAnne J.

Chapter One

A meadow on the South Downs proved to be an idyllic place for a picnic. The scents of a myriad wild flowers intermingled with those of pine trees. In a field nearby, cows munched on hassocks of green grass, their long tails flicking away buzzing flies.

Lady Isabella Winton, lounging on a blanket, could not believe what she was hearing. "Alex. How could you? You promised. I've waited four years - four years."

"Deuce Isa, don't get overset. I can hardly refuse can I?" Lord Fitzroy, the Earl of Standford spluttered, putting down his glass of champagne.

"What about the wedding, the arrangements, the guests? How could you?"

"I have no choice; General Maddeson expects me as his aide-de-camp in Brussels."

"You could say no - just this once. He knew of our nuptials; he's a guest for pity's sake."

Alexander rose to his feet, his arms outstretched to placate her. "Bonaparte escaped Elba; he's in France. The General's request is an honour I cannot refuse."

"Don't start talking about honor. You use that each time."

His eyes embraced her bosom heaving with anger. In two long strides, he grabbed her, drawing her close, intending to kiss her to silence.

Struggling she gasped, "Unhand me Alex, this time you will not win."

Smiling, he held her fast, "Look, I shall be back within a couple of months. I'm sure the countess will delay the nuptials?"

"Not again Alex. Dammit - let me go."

How dare he treat marriage so lightly, it was an insult to her and her family. "I can't forgive you for this. In fact I think I will call the whole thing off, tis too much."

Eyebrows raised, his sea blue eyes twinkling, he said, "Come on sweetheart, you know you don't mean it."

She grimaced; "I do and I will announce it as soon as we return. Now let me go."

His answer was to drag her down on the blanket, smothering her face with kisses. He felt her loosen against him, her lips quivering. Raising his head, he said, "I love you Isabella - we will be together - soon."

She willed herself not to give in; it would mean another year of waiting, another year without him. She had to fight him for this. Before their engagement, he'd been a rake of the first order. With his raven black hair dressed in the Brutus style, the curls framed a face that modeled a Grecian statue; God knows how many hapless girls he had seduced? However, on offering for her, he promised to remain faithful. Yet, even now, he may have a mistress installed in Brussels. "Married or not, I will go with you."

He raised his head, and sitting up, drew her to him. "No sweetheart, you know you cannot, besides, tis dangerous times, and I will not be around to protect you all the time."

"You have a mistress out there, haven't you?"

"Darling I am true to you - God knows why, with your temper."

"Temper? You call asking for my rights, temper? Besides, a couple of my friends are already out in Brussels having a grand time, dinners, the theatre, opera, and lavish balls. So I shall join them."

"I forbid it; I will not allow you to put yourself in jeopardy. In this, you will obey me."

Isabella's jade eyes narrowed. "What? Forbid? Not allow? Whom do you think you're addressing - some nincompoop?"

"Look I don't want to frighten you, but war is imminent. Women out there could lose their lives."

Pushing him away, Isabella rose to her knees, her hands

fisted on her hips. "Don't tell me what is not good for me. I will make my own choices. And, never - ever use that word obey again."

"I don't think the countess would approve, and as for your Papa, he knows there could be war. He will have an apoplexy."

"I am three and twenty years Alex; Papa respects my decisions. So do not use my parents as an excuse."

"Why are you so determined to come with me? If we went to war, our tent would be a tarpaulin slung on wooden posts. Is that what you want? Mud and putrid food."

"I know the tents to be otherwise. Why in the Peninsula wars, they lived in luxury, the tents even had a separate bedroom, so don't try and fool me."

Alex frowned, darn it; she was in a mood. "But my pet, there is so little time left to procure a house. Besides, there's the question of more servants, and a maid for you."

"I'm not your little pet - for God's sake treat me like a woman."

"Why I'll be pleased to do so." He lunged for her, pulling her to him.

Fighting him off, Isabella went for the kill. "In the Peninsula Wars, the wives stayed in the pensions or hotels. They watched the battles from the edge of the field."

"Gad, some of the ladies lost their lives, been mortally wounded. Even the other month, one of the wives dragged her husband off the field, and had half her head blown away by a canon."

Wincing, Isa poured herself a glass of champagne, "Well I haven't heard that particular story. Don't dramatize, Alex. I have made up my mind, if you are intent on going to Brussels, then I shall honour your decision, but I will go with you."

"Absolutely out of the question - now let us have no more of this nonsense. Pour me one will you?"

Duly filling his glass, she poured it over him. "Now listen to me Alex - I am coming, even if I have to run away and make for

Brussels alone."

"Honestly, you are a little hoyden. How pray are we to marry in four days?"

"Easily – a special license. You can manage that surely. Alex, I am going to Brussels, and that is an end to it."

"I repeat, no - definitely - no."

Isa looked at him. "You know it is useless to argue. There is no more to be said. We go together." Pouring him another glass of champagne, she said, "Alex - I love you; ache for you; I have been a virgin too long."

He took the glass draining it in one go. Putting it down on the tablecloth, he looked at the dark ringlets, tiny waist and curvaceous hips. She never ceased to arouse him. He edged up to her, ready to take her in is arms, kiss those full pouting lips.

She backed away. "We must marry forthwith. Papa will arrange that. However, it will be just us and the family."

He took a breath. "Well, thank the lord for that."

"Is that why you accepted the command, to escape the wedding nuptials?"

Lifting his glass, he smiled wryly. "To my lovely virgin - you win."

"Now to break the news to Mama – she'll have one of her fits." Her lips found his, her fingers curling into his long hair.

Groaning, in one swoop of his powerful arms, he pulled her onto his lap maybe marriage would be a good idea, he longed to do more than kiss her.

A Note from the Author

If you enjoyed this first chapter from A Lady's Plight (Lord of Sussex Series Book 1), you can find the whole book at Amazon. Please recommend and review the book.

About the Author

Katy Walters lives on the South Coast of England and loves to walk her golden retriever Lily along the beach. She is fascinated with the Regency and Medieval eras and enjoys visiting neighbouring Regency towns, researching for her books.

Contact

Katy Walters can be contacted at:
Twitter   **@katywalters07**
Facebook: **https://www.facebook.com/KatyWaltersAuthor**
Blog: **http://katywaltersnewsandviews.com/**
Blog 2.   **http://katysreviewsandnews.blogspot.co.uk/**
Website: **http://www.katy-walters.com**

Other books by Katy Walters

Regency Romance

A Lady's Plight
Lady Henrietta's Dilemma
Lady Phillipa's Peril
Lady Venetia's Vow

Historical Paranormal Romance

US   **Return to Rhonan**
US   **Possessed at Rhonan**
US   **Reunited at Rhonan**
Box-set of the complete trilogy coming soon

Crime – Mystery – Suspense – Thriller

Tortured Night: DCI Redd & DS Dove, Homicide Squad #1 in the Sussex Police Series
Splintered Moon : DI Samantha Templeton, Vice Squad #1 Sussex Police
Fractured Moon – DI Samantha Templeton Vice Squad, #2 Sussex Police Series. Coming Soon.

THE MARRIAGE LIST

by

AWARD-WINNING AND NATIONAL BESTSELLING AUTHOR

Dorothy McFalls

Copyright © 2014 Dorothy McFalls

Book Description

Compelled by his family to marry, Viscount Radford Evers makes a list of his requirements for a wife. Humble tenant May Sheffers meets none of these, so why does his heart beat madly at the sight of her?

Praise

Top 10 Bestselling Regency Romance for a year
Romantic Times Book Reviews Top Pick!

More Than 150 4 &5 Star Reviews

"Dorothy McFalls pens an enchanting, romantic historical that is sure to capture your heart. ... This is a heartwarming story filled with many twists and turns and is sure to be a favorite for any historical lover."

~ Romance Junkies

"The marriage list is an extraordinarily entertaining read....I whole heartedly recommend that the marriage list be placed on the very top of your list of "books to buy."

~ Cata Romance Reviews

Chapter One

Bath, England 1813

Radford, the fourth Viscount Evers, dismissed Bannor, his irritatingly efficient man-of-affairs, and eased his aching foot onto his study's massive tiger maple desktop. The wretched appendage throbbed like the devil all the way to the tips of his toes whenever the weather turned soggy. Which meant in dreary, sodden England his foot pained him nearly all the time. And the unrelenting patter of rain against the windowpane promised nothing but misery for the next several hours.

A year, three months, and twenty-five days had passed since his foot, his leg, and part of his chest had been crushed under the weight of his horse on the Peninsula. The days ticked by like the second hand on his father's weighty pocket watch he'd begun to twirl between his fingers.

"Taking this man-of-leisure lifestyle a little far, eh, Evers?" Lord Nathan Wynter intruded on Radford's self-loathing without the decency of an invitation. In fact, Wynter, Radford's fair-haired boyhood friend and the second son of the esteemed Marquess of Portfry, had burst into the study without even giving the Longbranch House's stoic butler the opportunity to deny him entrance.

Having awakened in a particularly aggravated mood, Radford had given his butler very specific instructions to turn all visitors away . . . especially Wynter.

For the past several days he'd shied away from prolonged visits with his friends. Wynter's presence served as an agonizing reminder of the healthy man he was before that cursed Frog murdered his horse out from under him in the middle of that miserable Battle of Salamanca. Not a day passed when he didn't long to turn back time and live as he once had—to savor the kind of reckless living Wynter freely enjoyed.

Days like today he felt as if he was nothing more than his injuries. Trapped.

His friend laughed, his ruddy cheeks brightening as he turned a deaf ear to Radford's vile curses and most ungrateful attempts to turn him away. There was no hope for it. Radford's foul mood only evoked a cheerier Wynter.

"Missed you at the Pump Room this morning." Wynter dropped into a heavily cushioned chair near the fireplace and plucked at the finely laced doilies covering the seat's wide arms.

A flare of anger surged in Radford's chest. "I've no interest in parading my lame leg around in public anymore. And those foul waters aren't doing a bloody thing." He folded his arms like a disobedient child and lifted his gaze to the ceiling. The blasted plaster needed repair.

"That tedious ritual of taking the waters is supposed to speed your recovery, Evers. But I had thought there might be another allure. A certain Lady Lillian Newbury noticed your absence. Her sunny smile faded to a petulant pout when she saw I was making the rounds alone." Wynter shivered dramatically. "Damaged my fragile male pride, she did."

Radford grimaced. Lady Lillian paid far too much interest in his recovery. Lovely as a spring flower, she followed him around the Bath events with the most piteous look clouding her crystal blue eyes.

He had no use for pity, especially not from a mere slip of a woman. Of course he'd no option in light of his recent revelation but play the grateful courtier to her demure interests. He'd do well to remember that damaged specimens such as himself weren't the choicest morsels on the marriage block.

Wynter didn't seem to mind Radford's brooding silence. His lips twitched while a wry look of amusement danced in his eyes. An outsider might say Wynter was on the verge of laughing at his friend. If he dared, Radford would boot him out on his ear. But he knew Wynter well enough to banish the thought. He trusted his friend as fiercely as Wynter trusted him.

"Since you seem to have planted yourself in my study, you might as well make yourself useful." Radford dashed a glance toward the liquor cabinet.

That was all the encouragement Wynter needed. He wasted no time in pouring two glasses of Radford's finest claret.

"Now tell me, Evers. What the devil has gotten into you today? You're a hundred score ruder than usual." Wynter sipped his claret and that look of amusement spread from his eyes to fill a good-natured grin. Only a long time friend would know Wynter planned to stand his ground and twist a confession from Radford's lips.

Radford steepled his fingers and frowned. He'd learned on the Peninsula the hard way that some battles were not worth fighting.

"Mother arrived last night."

"*Ah.*" Wynter leaned back in his chair and lazily propped one leg over the other.

"She's reminded me how close I came to facing my own mortality. Reminded me how I was carried home on a litter, insensible, and how the local vicar had been called upon to perform last rites no less than three times." He loathed the note of bitterness in his voice. Bitterness was below him, below the proud line of heroes he'd been born into.

"I suppose your loving mamma had a reason for dredging up that unhappy time from this past year?"

Radford nodded and then drained his glass. "She's reached the conclusion I myself have refused to face."

"Good Lord." Wynter took a deep sip of his own drink. "This sounds serious."

"It is serious. I have a responsibility to my family and my title that has been long neglected. In short, it is past time I get myself a wife and start producing heirs."

The very thought of tying himself to a flitting, muslin-draped, empty-headed lady for the rest of his days turned his

55

stomach.

"In all my experience," Radford said, "I've never known a woman to tax her silly mind long enough to think of anything beyond fashion, gossip, and the financial security only a man can provide."

"Gad, Evers, marriage can't be as bad as all that. We're talking about finding you a gently trained lady, not some harridan."

Radford sighed. Wynter was right. "I suppose it can't be worse than picking through the nags at Tattersall's to find a truly superior piece of horseflesh."

A blond brow rose. "Finding a wife isn't like purchasing a new mare for your breeding program."

"And why not? It *is* simply a breeding program I am looking to begin, is it not? Besides, what in blazes makes you an expert? You're blissfully unattached . . . with no plans to tie yourself up in the foreseeable future."

"True, true, I do try to avoid the curse of such an attachment," Wynter admitted with a lazy wave. "But a lady, Evers. Their natures are more sensitive than even your highest-strung Arabian. And ten times more unpredictable."

"Bah! I wish to make a list of qualities I should consider—a marriage list, I suppose. Make yourself useful for a change. Play the part of secretary."

"I don't know about this—" Wynter muttered.

"Just fetch a pen and a scrap of foolscap. I feel a burst of inspiration emerging."

~*~

"Oh please do stop fidgeting, Iona." The generally fearless May Sheffers thought her rebuke rang hollow even to her own ears. Especially when her heart was thumping in her throat. It took all her resolve not to pull out her lace handkerchief and tug it to bits, her nerves were so overset.

56

This is truly the only way.

The writ of eviction had arrived in the morning post. Luckily, May had caught sight of the letter and whisked the offensive missive from her ailing Aunt Winnie's frail fingers. The dear woman, who'd nurtured May from her fourth year forward, didn't need to know of the heartless treatment that wiry Mr. Bannor sought to bear upon them. Imagine, being tossed out of their home of the past two years like an unwanted pair of worn boots. She'd do anything to protect Aunt Winnie from having to worry about something as horrid as that.

May had spent the past month trying to solve the problem. She'd petitioned Mr. Bannor on several occasions to plead her case, only to find her explanations and promises of payment falling on ears made of stone. And that, along with the finality the writ of eviction presented, had forced May to take this outrageous course of action.

She had no other choice but appeal to the man who paid Mr. Bannor's salary, the owner of the small cottage she and Aunt Winnie currently rented. That was why she'd borrowed Iona's family carriage and was presently on her way to pay a call on the baffling Viscount Evers.

May could only pray Evers would sympathize with her plight.

"It's not as if we deliberately failed to pay the rent these past three months," May said sharply as the carriage swayed up Sion Hill toward their destination. Working up her ire helped sooth her jumpy nerves. "I never asked for Papa's money to be tied up by the courts. He's not dead! Neither is Mamma! Uncle Sires has gone too far. Trying to declare them dead just because he hadn't heard word from them for the past seven years, indeed. I remember a time when eight years passed between correspondences. They are busy with their investigations, Iona. Not dead."

"Yes, May," Iona said in her proper tone that always grew more subdued, more silent whenever May lapsed into one of her loud outbursts. "I am certain you are correct. But paying a visit on a gentleman and a bachelor? We don't even have a male escort, May. I wish you had allowed me to let my father handle this matter for you. Surely this action steps far beyond the bounds of—"

"Lady Iona Newbury. Do you or do you not still subscribe to the Mary Wollstonecraft school of thought?"

"I do. But—"

"And where does the indomitable Miss Wollstonecraft endorse handing our problems over to a man simply because we were born women?"

At that very moment, Iona's family carriage pulled to an abrupt stop, sending May's heart into another flutter of nervous activity. She fiddled a moment with her russet curls made impossibly unruly by the drenching weather. Her peacock blue walking dress, last year's muslin and design, was slightly faded, but neatly pressed. Her oilskin cape had a small rip in the shoulder.

May sighed. All and all, she looked her usual shabby self.

The carriage driver opened the door and held a large umbrella for the two women to huddle under as they walked along the flower-lined path up to the imposing Longbranch House entrance.

A pair of growling marble tigers stood guard on each side of the double doors. May swallowed a lump of anxiety before boldly knocking. When no one immediately opened the door, she was ready to breathe a sigh of relief and convince herself that the thoughtless Viscount Evers had fled to London or his country estate.

He hadn't taken the waters that morning. Iona's younger sister, Lady Lillian, had returned from the Pump Room in a sour mood after lingering far longer than either Iona or May in hopes he might appear.

He could have left Bath. Fashionable bachelors seldom lingered in a city that was turning into a haven for the elderly and the chronically dull.

The door opened a crack just as the women turned to leave.

"Yes?" A long-faced butler drawled. He frowned down his nose at the two ladies while they shivered in the damp air. Despite all that was courteous, he appeared dead-set against allowing either woman the opportunity to seek refuge inside.

His cold demeanor didn't dissuade May from her set path. It wasn't as if this was her first time facing down an uppity servant. Three weeks out of every year, May and Aunt Winnie visited her uncle Sires at his estate, Redfield Abbey in Wiltshire. And for those three dreadful weeks, the entire household of servants seemed to sneer down their noses and sniff in indignation whenever finding themselves in May's service. And never once did their disapproval overset her nerves.

Neither would this impertinent butler blocking the entrance to Viscount Evers' home. She narrowed her gaze and thrust Iona's and her own card into the butler's gloved hand. "I demand to see the viscount." A cruel smile curled her lips when he refused to budge. "I will stand out on this stoop and make a nuisance of myself in front of his neighbors if you dare deny me."

The butler grumbled something about having his head served on a platter before throwing open the doors. He took their cloaks, ushered the two women into a cozy parlor just off the grand pink marble entranceway, and then ambled off, still shaking his head and mumbling.

"The viscount won't agree to see us," Iona said as she flounced into a petite chair. "It wouldn't be proper."

"I believe you are correct." May left the warmth of the dainty parlor and followed the path the butler had taken. Iona, not one to ever be left behind, raised her skirts and ran with a hoyden's charm to catch up.

"Well, send them away," an angry male voice carried through the empty hall.

May couldn't make out the butler's reply, but she could

guess he was doing a valiant job pleading her case from the shouted exclamation that followed the short silence.

"Take up residence? That is ridiculous, Jeffers. I told you not to disturb me and here you are disturbing me yet again. Go away."

"He sounds like he's in a temper," Iona whispered.

"Naught but male bluster," May said, praying she was right. She held her breath and pushed open the closed door, having determined that the source of the angry voice resided within. Without waiting for a by your leave, she took Iona's hand in her own and marched into the leather-appointed study with her head held high, a solid army front.

"Pardon me for intruding," she said in the haughtiest tone she could muster, "but I must demand a word with you, my lord. It concerns a matter of importance that simply cannot be put off for another day."

Her sharp gaze landed on the viscount, lounging like a man who hadn't a care in the world with his booted foot propped on his lovely desk. He was a handsome devil.

Though they'd never been properly introduced, she'd seen him several times when she accompanied her aunt to the Pump Room. While Winnie leaned heavily on her arm as they took a turn around the room, nodding at familiar faces, May had caught her gaze straying more than once to the raven-haired gentleman with those arresting jade-colored eyes. He rarely stopped to converse with anyone.

She had watched as he'd stubbornly struggled to hide a severe limp and make his way around the Pump Room without the aid of a cane. Lord Nathan Wynter always accompanied the viscount, smiling and nodding to the young ladies while swinging the unused cane.

"Ladies." Lord Nathan leapt to his feet, nearly knocking over the small writing desk beside which he was sitting. He sketched a bow, a deep blush rising to his cheeks. May watched with interest as he hastily pushed a piece of foolscap into his pocket.

She wasn't surprised to find him here in the viscount's study. Bath was awash with gossip and speculation centering on Viscount Evers and how he begrudgingly accepted the support of his loyal friend Lord Nathan. One couldn't sit down in a tearoom without being bombarded with stories of how Evers received his injuries in the heat of a heroic battle and how he'd since become just a shadow of the bright, young rogue he used to be.

"Lady Iona Newbury and Miss Margaret Sheffers, my lord," the butler announced in a loud voice, as if he'd orchestrated May's and Iona's surprise appearance.

"Indeed," Viscount Evers drawled. His dark brows rose at least an inch. He studied the women several moments before lowering his foot from his desk. His jaw tightened as his foot dropped to the floor, the only hint his movement might have pained him.

May felt only the briefest frisson of guilt.

After all, *he* was responsible for his man-of-affairs, Mr. Bannor. And Bannor was the villain threatening to evict May and her dear Aunt Winnie from their home—no doubt with the viscount's blessing.

Evers fastened a hardened gaze on May as he rose from his chair. The pressure of his scrutiny wrecked havoc on her confidence until she noticed the reason for his unbreakable concentration. His hand stayed in contact with the desktop while he walked stiffly out from behind his artificial throne.

This wasn't a fearful force more powerful than the king. He was just a man fashioned, like her, from flesh and blood.

"Ladies." He gave a shallow bow. With a languid sweep of his perfectly manicured hand, he motioned to a small sofa by the fire grate. "Please sit and share this matter of business so urgent it supercedes all rules of propriety."

He smiled, flashing his teeth in a wholly unnecessarily aggressive move. The nerve of him, handing her not only a frosty set-down but also displaying a most egregious snarl. May

61

sucked in a breath and opened her mouth to return sharp words of her own, only her words wouldn't be couched in feigned politeness.

But alas, she needed to charm the man—not prick his nerves. With a sweet smile that was anything but real, May obediently perched on the edge of the sofa he'd indicated. Iona crowded next to her. Like a nervous bird, her friend shivered, which did nothing to bolster her own wearying nerves.

"Please fetch a pot of tea," Viscount Evers said quietly to the butler. Curiously, Wynter responded to the request with a nod and a playful wink.

What in heavens was going on? Never had May felt more like she'd stumbled into a den of lions. Perhaps the rules of propriety, deeming it unseemly for a woman to visit a bachelor in his home, were based on some very real danger. She felt her smile strain.

"Gentlemen, I sincerely appreciate your taking the time to receive us after we've practically stormed the gates."

"Practically?" The viscount's raven eyebrows jutted up again. The one word nearly exploded with sarcasm.

"Well, yes. I do apologize for my behavior. Lady Iona is only here because I wouldn't allow her to change my mind about seeing you, and she insisted I not make this visit alone." May swallowed her pride and kept her painful grin firmly in place. "I wouldn't have dreamed of disturbing you in this manner if there was any other way . . . "

His expression glowed with interest. He leaned against his desk and cocked his head. The fabric of his buff-colored superfine suit coat strained across his chest's wide expanse.

Oh my, she really shouldn't notice such things. She could be certain he wasn't noticing anything alluring about her person.

No man ever had.

She was worse than plain. Uncle Sires had judged her an ugly duckling with no hope of ever blooming into a swan. Aunt Winnie had protested the charge, but given May's ruddy hair, olive-tinged complexion, and rather stout shape, the dear woman didn't have much material to work with. *She has a heart of gold*, Winnie had finally concluded.

And no chance for attracting a husband. Uncle Sires' biting words had been spoken six years ago when May was barely eighteen and had excitedly inquired about her come-out. They still held power over her today. A heated blush rose up her neck.

She'd no right to look longingly upon a man as handsome as the Viscount Evers. No right at all. For all she knew, his stomach was churning from being forced to gaze upon a full-grown duck as unappealing as her.

His lightly arched brows furrowed and his glare grew impossibly hard. "If there was any other way . . . ?" he asked.

The question caught May off guard. What was he asking? Any other way, what? A growing blush stung her cheeks as she realized her overlong stare had interrupted her own explanation, mid-thought. His question must have merely been an attempt to prod her into talking and to bring her to the point.

"My aunt and I rent number twelve Sydney Place," she said.

His expression was as empty as a clear sky.

"You own the property," she prompted.

"Do I?"

For a moment May had a nervous feeling that she'd made a terrible mistake, that she'd intruded into the wrong man's home. "Mr. Bannor is your man-of-affairs, is he not?" she asked with a crisp tone.

"He is. He handles my assortment of properties and investments." Something dark and quite wicked crossed his brows. "Has Bannor offended you in some way, Miss Sheffers?"

May could not describe the relief that surged through her veins. "Indeed he has, my lord."

She peeled the writ of eviction from the silk reticule that matched her gown and held it out for him to take. "He has sent this. Luckily, I opened the letter before my aunt Winnie had a chance to read it. She's in poor health. Her heart. It was her ailing health that brought us to Bath from London, I'll have you know. A shock such as this would only worsen her condition."

"Indeed?" he drawled.

He took a moment then to read Bannor's letter. May held her breath as she counted the slow passage of seconds.

"The writ claims you and your aunt have failed to pay rent for the past three months," he said after more than two minutes of breathless silence. May was convinced she'd turned blue. "Is this true?"

"Yes, but—"

Evers cut her off with a staying hand. "This is a matter for Bannor, miss. I have no interest in squabbles of this sort. I don't interfere with my man-of-affair's occupation." His tone nearly coated the room with frost.

"Perhaps we could but listen to the women, Evers?" Wynter said, his gentle smile powerful enough to sway even the most stubborn of goats. "Surely, the task we were completing could only benefit from the experience?"

The viscount cast his friend a sidelong look. "No." He took several stiff steps, closing the distance between him and May. "We shall change the subject."

The long-nosed butler interrupted then with a tea tray. Steam rose from the finely hand-painted blue pot. An intricate scene depicting several maidens crossing an oriental bridge came to life on the porcelain. May couldn't help but wonder at the small fortune the viscount must have paid for the tea service as she silently poured the tea into the cups.

She took a long sip, a bounty of flavors filling her mouth. Her aunt's watery brew tasted like dirty hot water in comparison.

"A change of topics, then?" Wynter prompted after taking a sip of his tea as well. Mischief sparkled in his eyes.

May strangled the teacup's handle with a small measure of alarm. Perhaps the men were planning to make sport of the two foolish maidens like a scene out of a children's fable after all.

"I would rather—" she started.

64

At that very moment Viscount Evers blurted, "How old are you, Miss Sheffers?" He looked serious, too serious.

"Four-and-twenty. Now if you would please but listen."

"Is that on the shelf?" Evers turned and asked Wynter.

At least Wynter had the honor to drop his mouth open with embarrassment. "I don't believe so," he said, wincing. "Not quite."

"And horses, Miss Sheffers, what are your thoughts on them?"

The question was utter nonsense. Had the viscount's war injuries addled his mind? "I-I don't know, my lord. I've lived my entire life in London and don't know much about the creatures. They are rather *large* . . . imposing, I suppose."

He merely shrugged. "And you Lady Iona? How old are you?"

Iona, bless her, tilted her chin up like a true lady. "I am one-and-twenty, my lord, and by no means on the shelf. Neither is Miss Sheffers. My own mamma didn't marry until she was five-and-twenty, having to wait for my papa to come to his good senses."

Wynter tossed back his head and laughed boldly. "Very good, my lady."

The behavior of the two men, as if they shared a private jest at hers and Iona's expense, went beyond improper. Their idea of humor was just too much to bear. May felt at a loss. What should she do? Salvaging this confrontation with the viscount was clearly beyond hope. She sprang to her feet. Coming to his home was a mistake. A blot on her normally logical mind.

"My lords,"—she swept the room with her most menacing glare—"since you are unwilling to listen to my plight and help a gentlewoman in need, I believe I have no choice but to bring this farce to an end. Good day."

She snatched up Iona by the wrist and bolted from the room.

"It was truly a pleasure," Iona had the grace to call as they rushed out into the drizzly rains without the protection of their cloaks and worse . . . without having accomplished anything beyond making complete and utter fools of themselves.

"A pleasure, you say? Viscount Evers can take his cursed home with all its cursed expensive hand-painted fineries and go straight to the devil for all I care!"

Buy The Marriage List

Amazon

iBooks

Kobo

About the Author

For Regency and mystery author, Dorothy McFalls happily-ever-after is more than just a fictional ending, having enjoyed every day of marriage to her sexy sculptor husband. Formerly an environmental urban planner, she now writes full time. For information about Dorothy's upcoming books, visit her website at http://www.dorothymcfalls.com/

Dorothy also writes cozy mysteries as Dorothy St. James, including the White House Gardener Mystery series, which critics have called "spunky" and "fast-paced." Learn more about her mystery releases at http://www.dorothystjames.com/

Contact Me
Website: http://www.dorothymcfalls
Facebook: https://www.facebook.com/dorothy.stjames
Pinterest: http://www.pinterest.com/dorothystjames/

Other books by Dorothy McFalls

Lady Iona's Rebellion

The Nude: A Historical Romance

The Huntress

Lady Sophie's Midnight Seduction

Taken By Moonlight

A Wizard for Christmas

Neptune's Lair

Mystical Seduction

Birds in Paradise

Writing As Dorothy St. James

Flowerbed of State

The Scarlet Pepper

Oak and Dagger

LOVE IN A PAWN SHOP

by

NATIONAL BESTSELLING AUTHOR

Bonnie Edwards

Copyright © 2013 Bonnie Edwards

Book Description

A pit bull, a pawn shop and a pain-in-the-ass kid brother...

Dix is good with two out of three. She's had it with dusty shelves, desperate people and her teenage brother. With Riley about to graduate, Dix is ready to buy her one-way ticket to Paris.

Then sexy cop Dane Caldwell walks into her store on the hunt for stolen goods, and threatens her brother and her business.

The worst threat is to Dix's heart...if she loses that, she loses her dream.

Dane soon realizes he's found love in a pawn shop. Even the pit bull thinks he's okay. Now all he has to do is convince Dix that love is more than just another complication.

Praise

"The gamut of emotions, worry, fear, determination and most importantly she'll make you fall in love with her too sexy for a woman's good heroes... pick this one up. Because this one - You Gotta Read!"

~You Gotta Read Reviews.

"This fun and sweet Contemporary Romance with Bonnie Edwards' typical humor sprinkled throughout... anyone who loves category romance, or sweet romance with some spicy scenes will love this. . . .quite entertaining and a great way to pass a rainy afternoon."

~GotFiction.

Chapter One

Dane Caldwell ignored his better judgment at 3:45 p.m. and walked across the street into Dixon's Pawn Shop. Like millions of others in every city in America, the shop sat in a row of storefronts with overhead apartments. Except for the signs, they were all identical. Each one had a door at the side for the apartment stairwells, and he'd bet each one also had a rear entrance to the apartment from an alley in back.

Cops liked to know where the exits were, but since he was here without backup, he'd take the most direct approach and walk in like any other customer. He was so far out of his jurisdiction, he might as well be from Mars.

He'd watched the place since arriving from Philly this morning. But at 3:10 p.m. waves of school kids had begun to visit the store and he had to see for himself what drew them in. He didn't know much about children, but a pawn shop was a damn strange hangout for nine-year-olds.

Three boys went inside, and he slid in behind them and kept his back to the window as they barreled up to the counter in the darker recesses of the store. He planned to hang back and observe, nothing more.

Then he saw her.

Dark red hair fell in slight waves across her face. Her mouth, pursed in concentration, sat over a strong chin with a slight dimple. It had to be her. His information said she worked alone every weekday.

The woman must be Dix Dixon. She bent over her cash drawer with a screwdriver in her hand.

As the boys raced toward the counter, papers fluttered in

71

their hands. "Hey, Dix! We got our report cards! Wanna see?"

Her chin dimple disappeared when she smiled at the boys. Warm, friendly, and bright enough to clear the gray Seattle sky, her smile packed a punch. He narrowed his gaze as she patted each head affectionately and read their report cards in turn. Each boy preened at her compliments. Dane frowned. She could charm the birds from the sky.

And his grandmother out of the family jewels. For a woman like Dix, conning an old lady would be a piece of cake.

The boys were busy petting some kind of animal; from where he stood, he couldn't tell if it was a cat or dog.

Dane hung back, surprised that a woman he was half convinced was a con artist would give this kind of attention to neighborhood kids. He supposed that her wide-open smile worked its magic on most people. It was certainly working on him. He fought the urge to smile along with the boys and feigned interest in a carpenter's tool kit. He'd given in to his curiosity and come into the shop, but he wasn't idiot enough to move closer.

"I'll be right with you," she said to him. After one more set of oohs and ahs, she handed the boys back their report cards.

He gave her a nod and studied the front of the store while listening to the conversation behind him. Older computers, household appliances, and sports equipment filled the front half of the space. Closer to the counter, he saw electric and acoustic guitars hanging from the ceiling. Amplifiers lined the walls.

She clapped her hands, pulling his attention to her again. She said, "Okay, troops, line up single file and head for the exit. I've got work to do."

The boys groaned and she grinned at them. When they turned, he could see them better. Identical triplets.

"Now," she said. "If you see my brother, tell him to get his butt home. I want to see how he did on his science quiz."

"Ah, Dix," one of them said, "Quit worrying. Riley's gonna make it. All the way."

72

"Yeah," the other two chimed in. "All the way, Riley, all the way, Riley!" they chanted until she whistled loud enough to be heard over the din.

"Like I said, line up and get a move on." She clapped her hands again to shoo them along.

The boys trooped past him single file until they reached the door. Then they jammed up, arms and legs and elbows wedging their way through.

He was hard-pressed not to laugh, but he managed. He wasn't here to be amused. He was here to get an overall impression of the woman.

As soon as the boys squeezed their way out the door, he was alone with her.

Center stage.

~*~

Dix's day was going pretty well. And now she had an honest-to-God browser by the front of the store. After the Fanelli boys had squeezed their way out the door, she sized up the stranger as best she could. He stood with his back to the window, so she couldn't make out his face. His silhouette was imposing, but that didn't faze her.

At her size, not many people intimidated her physically, and in her profession, she met a lot who tried.

He stepped closer and out of the window's glare. He was broad in the shoulders. Good looking, too. "And what can I do for you, Good Lookin'?" She flashed her best shopkeeper's smile. It wasn't like her to use flirtatious talk, but it had just popped out.

That's what happened when she spent too much time alone.

The stranger's all-encompassing gaze said 'cop,' but she knew all the locals and didn't recognize him. "You must be new around here," she said in a questioning tone, which he ignored.

He trailed a finger over an amplifier as he moved closer. He leaned over to give it a better look, and she drew in a breath at his profile. Strong nose, commanding chin, high-ridged brow bone. She'd been right: this was one good looker.

"Just browsing," he said in a smoky blues club voice. She had an ear for voices, and his was strong and warm with just a hint of rasp that could, if she let it, trail down her spine. She closed her eyes to help her absorb the sound and let it slide to her vitals. Mm-mm. Fine.

She suddenly remembered she was alone in the store, except for Razor, who only looked like a nasty dog. He was still in a happy stupor from the kids petting him. She slanted him a glance and toed him in the side. He lifted his head and cocked it. She clicked her tongue and he stood without a sound.

This man had waited for the boys to leave so they would be alone. She hated when that happened.

She idly placed her right hand over the screwdriver she'd been using on the stuck cash register drawer and cupped her other hand over the panic button just under the counter.

She studied him. His new leather jacket said he wasn't likely a junkie or a robber. Still, he walked with deliberation toward her. Observation, honed by years of practice, told her he never moved quickly. If he were a buyer, he'd be decisive once he found the item he wanted. He would go after anything he wanted. And get it.

Warmth bloomed deep in her chest as she watched him raise his face to the ceiling to study the guitars. She'd been right about his chin.

Razor leaned against her calf and jutted his head around her leg. He peered through his lookout hole in the counter's swinging door. She could handle just about anyone with Razor at her side.

She knew the exact moment when the man noticed the dog.

Razor wasn't what anyone would call 'cute.' The black and white pit bull was scarred and marked by abuse with one ear half chewed off. Most people stopped dead at sight of him.

Not this guy. His step faltered for a split second, but when

Razor didn't bark or growl, he continued to move toward her.

Which she decided was a sign of character.

Razor continued to watch him but must have seen even less threat than she did, because his tail soon thumped against her leg.

She wanted to see the man's eyes, but the instruments overhead shadowed his face. Thanks to Paul, her part-timer, she did a brisk business in guitars and amps.

The browser hadn't said anything more, but a lot of people wanted to be left alone. Good, he wouldn't waste her time with useless questions. Once he saw something he wanted, he'd ask only the pertinent stuff.

She considered going back to work on the cash drawer, but couldn't force her eyes away from his easy grace. His grin showed straight teeth and eye crinkles. She gauged his age at around thirty-five, give or take a year. She couldn't make out the color of his eyes, but he was gorgeous. Her breath wheezed out at the sight of his ring-free left hand. "May I help you find something?"

Not that she was in the market for a man, because she'd run for the hills if one asked her out, but still, good looking and single added a touch of spice to her day.

"No, thanks," he replied to her offer of help, "I haven't been in before and wanted to check the place out." He looked at the guitars threatening to brain him. His eyes caught and lit up. "Is that a Fender Mustang?"

"Hand made in '65," she replied, easing her grip on the screwdriver.

"Nice." He looked around again, but kept Razor in his peripheral vision. Smart, too. She liked smart men.

So few of them came into the store that this one stood out. Who was she kidding–he'd stand out anywhere.

"You're a musician?" she prodded, wanting to hear him use that voice again. There was no harm in chatting, because he'd leave soon and wouldn't return. Smart men with great teeth and new leather coats never did.

"Nah, I just did the garage thing when I was a kid. But a buddy of mine had a Mustang. He told me Jimi Hendrix used one in the studio."

His gaze wasn't on the guitar now but on her. Her belly dropped hard, like an egg into a hot frying pan. Ker-splat. Sizzle.

A shaft of primal awareness steamed up her spine. She couldn't for the life of her remember the conversation. Her face heated and she blinked, trying to come up with something, anything, to say to cover the full silence. In the end, all she could do was stare and remind herself that she wasn't in the market for a man. Not now!

He reached up and smoothed his hand across the guitar's finish, reminding her of what they'd been bantering about.

"Yes, Jimi did use a Mustang, but only for one album. He liked the whammy bar. I doubt it was that one, though." She leaned her elbows on the counter and gave him her cheekiest smile. "But I could tell you it was if that'd make a sale for me."

He grinned again, all sex and male interest. His gaze dropped to her cleavage and back to her eyes. Her temperature rose with his eyes.

Trouble. Six feet four inches of trouble.

Sexy trouble, fun trouble, and the kind of trouble she hadn't had in a long, long while. The kind she couldn't afford now.

Razor picked that moment to send a waft of pure stink into the room. His opinion stated, he groaned and circled at her feet until he landed with a thud. Clearly, he didn't see the harm this man was doing to Dix's equilibrium.

"Oh, man! My eyes are watering," he said as he backed up out of harm's way. "What are you feeding that dog?" He waved his hand in front of his face.

Empathy enveloped her and she turned on the ceiling fan. "This will help."

But the moment was ruined, and he looked at his watch and backed away. "I'm late," he said, and walked to the exit, his head

76

turned to see the contents of the jewelry case as he cruised by.

"Too bad you didn't find anything you liked," she said to his retreating back. For a moment there, she'd thought he had. She supposed it was a good thing he'd had a look around and wouldn't return.

He left without a backward glance. Just as well, because men like him were dangerous. She had no time for dangerous men. Especially not men who looked like him– all sex and hard lines. If she got involved with a man like him now, it would ruin everything.

And nothing–but nothing–would ruin her plans; not a man, not sex, not a sexy man, not a man with sex on his mind, not even a smart man with sex on his mind.

She checked the time. Here it was after four and still no sign of Riley. She tried a practice conversation in her mind, a dialogue in which they actually communicated. Hey, sis. How was your day? Tolerable, she'd answer, and they'd play a hand of gin rummy the way they used to. They'd laugh the way they used to. Have fun the way they used to, and she'd be his big sister again instead of the nagging bitch she'd become.

In her wildest imagination, she couldn't see it happening.

She sighed. She loved her brother, would do anything to help him through these teen years, but most days he was a pain in the butt.

She picked up a pile of mail. Mostly flyers and junk mail, but then she found the letter. Her heart stopped. The school in Paris.

She sucked in a breath. Held it to a count of three then let it whoosh out again.

Paris.

L'école Poirot and the life she'd been meant to live. The life that Fate had taken from her when her dad was shot. She blinked twice to force away her terrific sense of loss and injustice, and tore open the envelope.

"It was with great surprise that I read your letter,

Mademoiselle Dixon. I remember the tragic events that prevented you attending your final year of school here." It went on in a sympathetic tone until Dix wanted to scream, but she read every word.

She was hired.

An American housemother would bring an interesting element to the students' lives, the letter said. It was imperative she be ready to start work on September first. Her legs gave way and she sank to the floor, where Razor did his best to crawl into her lap. He licked her face and wriggled against her. She draped her arms around him and cried against his bony head.

September first. Only four months. Riley would be in university as long as he got that scholarship.

And she had to find a home for Razor. The thought of losing him in the midst of all her dreams coming true brought tears to her eyes. It didn't matter that she let them fall. Razor kissed them away.

A Note from the Author

If you enjoyed this first chapter from Love in a Pawn Shop, you can find the whole book at various retailers. Please recommend and review the book.

About the Author

Bonnie Edwards lives with her husband and pets on the rainy coast of British Columbia. She believes life should be lived with joy. That joy shows up in her earthy, irreverent love stories. Bonnie uses long hikes to bounce ideas off her husband and her standard poodle, who almost always agrees with her.

She has written novels, novellas and short stories for Carina Press, Harlequin, Kensington Books and Robinson (UK) although now she publishes her work herself.

Sometimes her stories have a paranormal twist, likes curses and ghosts, other times not. But they're always entertaining and guarantee a happy ending.

Contact

For more info and to sign up for her newsletter, check out her website: http://www.bonnieedwards.com/ and Amazon author page: http://www.amazon.com/Bonnie-Edwards
Find her on social media:
Twitter: https://twitter.com/BonnieEdwards
Facebook: www.facebook.com/Bonnie.Edwards.Author
Pinterest: https://www.pinterest.com/bedwards1342/
Goodreads:
www.goodreads.com/author/show/283636.Bonnie_Edwards

Other books by Bonnie Edwards

Erotic Romance:

Tales of Perdition (series)
Perdition House Part 1 An Erotic Saga
Perdition House Part 2 An Erotic Saga
Rock Solid (Tales of Perdition 3)
Parlor Games (Tales of Perdition 4)

Body Work
Slow Hand
Stroke of Midnight

Contemporary Romance:

Sweet Ride!
Possessing Morgan
Long Time Coming (A Short Romance)
The Stone Heart (A Short Romance)

RETURN OF THE RUNAWAY BRIDE

by

USA TODAY BEST SELLING AUTHOR

Donna Fasano

Copyright © 2011 Donna Fasano

Book Description

Once upon a time...there lived a lovely young woman named Savanna who was engaged to Daniel, a handsome law student. Theirs was to be a fairy-tale wedding. But Savanna's second thoughts were too big to be ignored, so the would-be bride ran away.

As the years passed...Daniel's heart turned to ice. It is this unfeeling man that Savanna faces upon her return. The love of her youth is now a stranger. Could Savanna ever make Daniel understand why she abandoned him? And could she convince the man of her dreams he will always be her Prince Charming?

Praise

"So what did I think about these characters? Spot-on!"
~Misty Baker, A KindleObsessed Review

"I highly recommend this book if you are looking for a sweet and realistic love story."
~The Autumn Review

Prologue

"I need to slip down to the kitchen to check with the caterer. I'll be right back to pin on your veil. I won't be two minutes, promise." The woman hesitated at the door and gazed warmly at her daughter. Sudden emotion glistened in her eyes. "Oh, honey, you're going to make a beautiful bride."

Savanna Langford watched the door of her bedroom close as her mother bustled out and then she took a deep, calming breath. Sitting down on the very edge of her bed so as not to crease the delicate double galloon lace covering her wedding gown, Savanna looked around the room that had sheltered both her and her dreams for all nineteen years of her life.

The pale-green spread covering the bed was sumptuous and soft. The matching curtains ruffling in the gentle breeze allowed the perfect amount of sunlight to shine through the open window. White bookshelves held all the classic novels that should be read by a proper young woman. Everything surrounding her was neat, tidy, pristine. This was a perfect room, in a perfect house, where she'd spent her perfect youth growing up in a perfect world.

And now the next phase of her life was soon to unfold before her. She was about to take part in the perfect wedding and marry the perfect man.

That Daniel Walsh III was the perfect man was no secret. Everyone said so. Danny was loving, caring, kind and gentle. Not only that, but Miz Ida, owner of Watson's Kwik-E Mart, adamantly declared that he was the most handsome man in the county. And Savanna's father had boasted on more than one occasion that Danny would be an excellent provider once he finished his final year of law school and passed the bar. Yes, everyone agreed that Danny Walsh was the best catch in town.

Savanna tipped her chin high and stared at the ceiling. "So

what's wrong with me?" she murmured. She knew Danny was perfect, that was one reason why she loved him with all her heart and soul. She'd never met another man like him.

Why, then, when she was about to embark on a lifelong journey with the man of her dreams, was she plagued with such doubt? Why, on what should be the happiest day of her life, did she feel as if she were being followed by an ominous thunder cloud?

There was no denying the dark cloud. It had been hanging over her head now for two full weeks.

She stood and paced the length of the room, twisting the fingers of both hands together this way and that.

"It's *nerves*," she said in a firm, loud voice. "It's only nerves. Put it out of your head."

Pressing a fist against her solar plexus, Savanna forced the tension from her trembling stomach and the distressing questions from her mind.

"Here I am." Savanna's mother rushed into the room, stopped and flattened her palm against her chest. "Oh, my. I need to slow down and take a breath."

A tender smile pulled at Savanna's mouth at the sight of her mother. "I know how hard you're working to make this a wonderful day for me, Mom," she said.

It was so like her mother to overwork herself. Each and every birthday was made special, each holiday an elaborate affair, because Mrs. Langford fussed to make everything perfect for her husband and only child.

Savanna's mother dismissed the compliment with a wave. "It's what being a mother is all about, honey. Now come. Sit." She patted the cushioned chair facing the mirrored vanity and fluffed the skirt of Savanna's gown after her daughter sat down.

"You should see Danny." The woman's blue eyes twinkled. "He looks so handsome in his tux. That black suit brings out the best of his dark good looks." Smoothing her hand along one side of Savanna's blond, upswept hair, she commented, "It's a shame your friends couldn't be here for the wedding."

"Maggie and Sharon left for school two weeks ago," Savanna said, a flash of sadness rushing through her at the thought of her friends who were now on the other side of the country. "And Josie was lucky to get an internship at that pharmaceutical company. With everyone just getting settled, it was too much to ask them to fly home again."

Mrs. Langford cocked a wicked eyebrow at her daughter's reflection. "Well, if they could see Danny today, they'd simply swoon."

Savanna laughed. "Swoon? Mom, no one 'swoons' anymore."

"Oh, yes, they do." Her lips quirked in a perky smile. "They just call it something else."

Savanna thought her mother was probably right; if her friends had been sitting downstairs, they most likely would have been swooning at the sight of Danny in a tux. But then the sight of Danny, no matter what his attire, had driven her high school friends crazy ever since he'd first shown an interest in Savanna. Maggie would consistently turn three shades of red, and Sharon would giggle herself silly. Josie, on the other hand, had always been pea green with envy because Savanna was involved with a "college man."

And now those same friends she'd graduated with were off seeking their destinies at colleges and corporations across the country. A small frown creased her brow as the black cloud of doubt billowed and thickened and hovered closer than ever.

"Oh, I forgot to tell you. Danny's parents arrived while I was downstairs." Savanna's mother gently shook out the folds of the gossamer veil. "They're with your father. I've never seen Daniel and Susan happier. And your father's floating around down there with a smile on his face that's a mile wide."

As she watched the reflection of her mother arranging the white, lacy panels of French silk tulle over her head, Savanna struggled to breathe. She supposed this match between herself and Danny had been a given from the very beginning...to her friends, her parents, Danny's family, even to Danny himself. And that had never bothered her before. So why did she find the thought so claustrophobic now?

Mrs. Langford positioned the stiff, satin-covered band on her daughter's head and began to pin it securely in place.

"You're going to make a wonderful wife," she said. "And your father and I can't wait to be grandparents."

But Savanna wasn't listening; she was concentrating on sorting out the feelings churning inside her.

Danny's attentions had always flattered her, had always made her feel special. His touch excited her, his kisses made her tremble. Being with him, she felt protected and secure. Danny would keep her safe, just as safe as she'd always been here at home, living with her parents.

As if she were a mind reader, Mrs. Langford said, "After today you'll have no worries." Her mother chattered on, not noticing Savanna's silence. "As the wife of a lawyer, your future will be set. I can't find the words to express just how happy I am. This is what your dad and I always planned for you."

As the words echoed in her head, Savanna's mind reeled. Her eyes widened a fraction as a realization struck her with force—everything had been planned for her. Every single aspect of her life had been mapped out by those who loved her. She'd always been sheltered, kept perfectly safe from the outside world. Never had she been touched by unpleasantness of any kind, never had she faced a problem alone.

Savanna struggled to remember one time in all her nineteen years when she had encountered and tackled an obstacle on her own, one time when she had overcome a challenge single-handed. The fact that she couldn't recall even one instance was mind-boggling.

"Mother..." Savanna's voice was raspy with dry emotion. "I can't do this."

Mrs. Langford continued to fuss with the headpiece. "Can't

do what, honey?" she asked blithely.

"I can't marry Danny."

"Of course you can." For several seconds, Mrs. Langford kept pinning the delicate veiling material, but Savanna's prolonged silence made her glance up. After studying her daughter's expression, she must have read the panic there, for her tone changed dramatically as she straightened and asked, "What do you mean you can't marry Danny?"

Savanna squeezed her eyes shut. "I don't know what I mean. It's hard to put in to words. I'm feeling something, and I'm not sure what it is." Her eyes were pleading for understanding when she looked up. "Something just isn't right."

"Don't be silly," her mother reproved. "You love Danny."

Twisting around to face her mother, Savanna said, "Of course I love him. He's wonderful."

"He is," her mother agreed, her voice suddenly tight. "And he'll take care of you. It's what your father and I want for you. It's what everyone wants for you, Savanna."

But was that what she wanted for herself? For someone to care for her for the rest of her days? The questions whirled inside her head, and Savanna was surprised by the tears that prickled her eyelids.

By marrying Danny was she merely fulfilling everyone else's expectations of what was best for her? If she did marry him, how would she ever know what she, Savanna Langford, was capable of achieving? How would she know what challenges might be awaiting her out in the world?

Who am I? she wondered. What do I want for myself? The questions rocked her to her very foundation. She had never asked that of herself before.

She might not know the answers to any of the questions that were rearing up in her mind, but she did know that she couldn't possibly commit herself to Danny until she had the chance to at least ponder them.

Immediately she reached up and began pulling at the pins

that held the headpiece in place.

"Savanna, stop that," her mother demanded.

The two of them engaged in what would have been a comical bout, as one plucked out hairpins and the other tried to snatch the pins and put them back into place. But there was nothing funny about the despair pushing Savanna to the brink of hysteria.

"Mother!" Frustrated by the game, Savanna stood so quickly the chair toppled over.

Mrs. Langford scowled. "You're being silly, Savanna. This is nothing but an attack of pre-wedding jitters." She stooped down and picked up the pins that had fallen to the floor. "It's usually the groom who gets cold feet."

"I cannot do this." Savanna's unflinching gaze made it evident that she was utterly serious.

Mrs. Langford stood and planted her hands on her trim hips. "The minister has arrived. The guests are assembled. Everyone is waiting for the bride's entrance." She cocked her head. "The bride is *you*, Savanna."

Savanna swallowed and tipped up her chin a fraction. "I need to talk to Danny."

Mrs. Langford's lips pursed so tightly that they paled under her sheer lipstick. After a long, tense moment, she said, "All right. I'll go find him. I only hope he can talk some sense into you."

After the door closed firmly, leaving her alone with her doubts and questions, Savanna wondered what on earth she was going to say to Danny. How could she explain her feelings? How could she make him understand when she didn't understand herself?

Fear and confusion gripped her with an icy hand and she buried her face in her open palms. "What are you doing?" she murmured.

There was a soft knock at the door. "Savanna?"

A familiar warmth rippled through her at the sound of

Danny's deep, rich voice.

"Danny!" Her urgent whisper was nearly choked off by a sob as she pulled open the door.

The very sight of him calmed her and she drank in the comfort his presence never failed to give. The smile that tilted his lips gave her strength and she tried valiantly to return a smile of her own.

"You're beautiful," he said. "But with all the superstition about bad luck, are you sure it's safe for me to see you before the ceremony?"

His jesting tone told her that he didn't realize the extent of her emotional state. Maybe it was better that he didn't know the turmoil she was feeling. What she needed to do was explain to him in clear, logical terms the chaos that was twisting around in her brain. The contradiction in terms nearly made her laugh aloud. Instead she took a deep breath.

"Danny," she began. It hurt to say his name, knowing what she was about to tell him. "I'm afraid I can't do this."

He took her hands in his and held them securely. The feel of his skin on hers was stirring. All she wanted to do was drift deeper into his protective embrace. No, her mind screamed. Not now.

"Savanna, everything's going to be all right. You'll see, as soon as we..."

His voice trailed off as she began to shake her head. She pulled her hands from his grasp and stepped back. She couldn't touch him and think clearly at the same time.

"You don't understand," she said. "I'm afraid."

"I know you are."

She saw his dark eyes fill with compassion and love.

God, why can't I get this right? 'Afraid' wasn't the word she'd meant to say. Anxiety swept through her, settling in the pit of her stomach where it churned, slowly and steadily.

"Listen," he said, "I'll go down and tell everyone that we need some time." He reached out and gently cupped her elbow.

"Say, an hour? That will give us time to talk." He chuckled. "Time for us to gather up your courage."

"But-"

"It's okay," he told her. "Dad can break open the champagne early. There'll be no harm in that, now will there?" He gave her a charming, lopsided grin.

Hope budded like a rose inside Savanna. Looking at Danny so confident and assured, she wondered how she had ever doubted that he couldn't make everything right.

He went over and uprighted the chair, leading her with him. "Now you sit down and relax." He settled her in the seat, leaned close and caressed her cheek with his strong, smooth fingers. "It's going to be all right, Savanna. I promise."

His lips were warm and moist as he pressed them against hers. "I'll be right back with a glass of bubbly." He grinned. "And then I'll remind you of all those dreams we made. That'll ease your nerves." He kissed her softly on the mouth.

When Savanna was alone she sat in the warm cocoon of security in which Danny had left her wrapped. She didn't need to worry. Everything was going to be just fine, perfect even.

Those two tiny words sent an icy prickle chasing up her spine. The shadowy cloud of apprehension that descended was thick enough to smother her.

"Oh, God!" The words ripped from her throat like a torturing claw as she ran toward her closet and wrenched out the suitcase she'd so carefully packed for her two week honeymoon.

She snatched the bridal veil from her head, barely wincing as the pins snagged then pulled free from her hair. She reached behind her to rip at the back of her gown, and a dozen dainty pearl buttons bounced soundlessly on the plush carpet.

~*~

Six years later...

90

Welcome to Fulton, Virginia. The wooden sign was weathered, but the letters were bright with fresh paint. Savanna had been in high school when the town council had voted to create the quaint welcome area with its cheery greeting and evergreen shrubs. She remembered that the Ladies' Auxiliary had always been responsible for manicuring the mound, and the crimson begonias and deep purple petunias were proof that the Ladies were still taking the job seriously.

As she crossed the town limit, Savanna released one hand from the steering wheel and reached up to massage her neck. Ever since she'd decided to return to her hometown, trepidation had coiled inside her tighter and tighter. It had been six years since she'd left behind everything important in her life—her friends, her family, the man she loved.

As she passed familiar scenes—the Bowl-A-Rama, Garvy's Service Station, Bob's Barber Shop with its red-and-white swirled column still spinning—the years melted away until it could have been just yesterday that she'd driven out of town as if the hounds of hell were on her scent.

Savanna stopped at the red light and closed her eyes. She shivered in spite of the warm, southern sun as icy doubt brought cold, realistic questions. Would the folks in town welcome her with open arms? Or turn their backs on her because of "the big scandal," as Savanna had come to name that episode of her life? The older residents worried her most, the ones whose memories were sure to be razor sharp and as clear as the lenses in their reading glasses.

And how would Daniel and Susan Walsh respond to her return? Would they see her long enough for her to explain her reasons for running away from marrying their son? They had to, Savanna thought. They simply had to.

Danny flashed into her mind and a band of apprehension tightened across her chest. How on earth was she ever going to face him?

A Note from the Author

If you enjoyed these opening scenes of Return of the Runaway Bride, you can find the book at these fine stores: Kindle Store, Nook Book Store, Kobo Store, iBook Worldwide, Google Play

About the Author

Donna Fasano is a USA TODAY Bestselling Author whose books have sold nearly 4 million copies worldwide and translated into 2 dozen languages. She's written over 30 romance and women's fiction titles that have made both the Kindle and Nook Top 100 lists numerous times.

Contact

Sign up for my newsletter and/or join my Street Team, The Prima Donnas, at www.DonnaFasano.com. Also, feel free to write to me via the "contact" tab on the website. I love to hear from my readers!

Facebook: www.Facebook.com/DonnaFasanoAuthor
Twitter: www.Twitter.com/DonnaFaz
Pinterest: www.Pinterest.com/DonnaFaz

Other books by Donna Fasano

Reclaim My Heart
The Merry-Go-Round
Mountain Laurel
The Single Daddy Club Series
Where's Stanley?
An Almost Perfect Christmas
And other titles

KISS ME, DANCER

Dance 'n' Luv Series
Book One

by

USA TODAY BEST SELLING AUTHOR

Alicia & Roy Street

Copyright © 2011 Alicia Street, Roy Street

Book Description

Ballet teacher Casey Richardson is all too familiar with hard times and disappointment. After years of struggle, she's on the verge of losing her beloved dance academy. Enter handsome playboy businessman Drew Byrne. The sexy divorced dad would fix things with a check if she'd let him. After all, Casey's the only person who's been able to reach his shy, withdrawn son. But will saving her school mean losing her heart?

Praise

"Simple AH-MEH-ZING...so much depth, emotion, passion and love...Hats off to the Streets for their beautifully written story of real life troubles and heartaches. A brilliant script for a chick flick we girls would love to cry and swoon about!"
~Unputdownable Books

"This story has the perfect amount of giggles, gasps, and anxious page-turning."
~Lost in Literature

Chapter One

Casey Richardson stopped correcting the drooping hands and unpointed feet of her nine- and ten-year-old students doing ronde de jambes at the barre when a man barged into her sunny mirrored studio, interrupting her Saturday morning ballet class.

A man who just happened to resemble a Greek god walking the earth in jeans and silky black tee. She ignored the flush of heat going through her at the sight of this hunk and said, "Excuse me, sir, but we have a class in session."

He shot Casey an impatient glance, stunning her with teal blue eyes. Grabbed little Josh by the arm and tugged him toward the lobby.

She'd seen Josh's parents at the last dance recital, and this guy definitely was not one of them. "Wait a second," Casey said, trying to cut him off as he made his way from the studio. "What do you think you're doing?"

He stepped past her.

The classroom of students fell silent. Casey turned to them. "Same drill. Ronde de jambes. Let's go." She nodded to Jiao at the piano. Her accompanist went into Chopin's Waltz in C-Sharp Minor.

Casey raced out to the lobby after the man (trying not to notice he had the most splendid back she'd ever seen). Timid Josh gave him no resistance but looked like he was about to cry.

"Lisa, block the door." The eighteen-year-old intern at the desk just sat there wide-eyed, unprepared for the sudden call to arms.

But Casey wasn't about to let some pervert make off with one of her precious flock. As the hunk reached for the door handle she slipped in front of him, her back to the door, her palms pressed like stop signs against his chest. She told herself

95

she didn't notice the hard curve of muscle beneath her hands. Or that his face looked even better up close. "Hold it or I'll call the police. Who are you, and what do you want with Josh?"

He gave her a cocky smirk, shifted his focus to her low-cut leotard and continued down her body with an assessing gaze. Casey practically lived in tights, but she suddenly felt undressed and exposed. She dropped her hands.

He murmured, "And who are you?"

His challenging tone struck an old chord of self-doubt deep within Casey. After so many years of not quite fitting anywhere and seeing everything she tried go up in smoke, she'd begun calling herself "Calamity" Richardson. But at twenty-eight the hard-won accomplishment of running her own studio gave her a chance to silence that internal voice.

And after the troublesome letter she received this morning, Casey already had enough on her plate without letting some dude reeking in attitude come marching in from nowhere with an intimidating side dish of his own bad day.

"I'm Casey Richardson, director of North Cove Dance Academy. And you are?"

"I'm his father. So don't go all rabid on me, pixie."

"Josh, do you know this man? Tell me the—"

Mr. Handsome cut her off. "You want my ID? Or maybe you need a sample of my DNA?"

"I want to hear from Josh."

"He's my other dad," the boy said sheepishly.

The man snorted. "*Other* dad? I'm his *real* father. Now let's go, Josh."

"Except, Dad, I've got to change my clothes."

Coming out of his agitated state, Josh's father seemed to finally look at the boy, who still wore tights and ballet slippers. "Oh. Okay. Go ahead."

He turned those keen blue eyes onto Casey once more as Josh ran off. "Don't tell me you never noticed his last name is different from his mother's."

96

Oops. Casey suddenly remembered that Josh's mom and the man she'd seen her with at the dance recital introduced themselves as the Wentoffs, but the boy was registered as Josh Byrne. "I'm so sorry. Then you must be..."

"Drew Byrne." He said it with the air of someone used to impressing people with his name.

Was she supposed to recognize him from somewhere? A lot of her students had wealthy, sometimes famous parents. "Um, yes, of course. I forgot about—"

"Forgot, huh? Guess all those pirouettes make you kind of dizzy."

She wanted to belt him. "I was trying to protect your son from a stranger who came rudely stomping unannounced into the middle of my ballet class. Normally when a parent needs to contact their child during class they simply go to the desk, and Lisa or someone else in charge will come to me."

The self-important Mr. Byrne wasn't even listening. He was gazing around at the dance academy's humble waiting lobby that probably looked to him as if it were decorated by the Salvation Army. Which wasn't far from the truth, since the worn green sofa and armchair came from her late grandmother's cellar.

But Casey didn't appreciate being treated like some irritating gnat. She gritted her teeth, fuming inside. "Mr. Byrne, I'm sure you wouldn't want me barging into your office while you're..."

He stepped so close her voice shrank to nothing. She could feel the heat coming off his diesel-cut frame. His warm skin smelled of soap and sandalwood and something incredibly male. He was at least a head taller than Casey, and when he looked down, a lock of sun-streaked sand-colored hair fell across his brow. "If you're dressed like that, Ms. Richardson, it might be fun."

Uh-oh. Maybe it was better being an overlooked gnat. She controlled the shiver in her body but couldn't stop the blush flaming her cheeks. This was clearly a man who knew how to play women. "What I mean is next time—"

"Won't be a next time. Josh isn't coming back."

"What? Is his mother aware of this? She told me Josh loved his classes here. It's good exercise for him. And he's exceptionally talented."

"I'm not often in the neighborhood to keep an eye on what's going down with Josh, but there is no way I'll let Heather or you turn my son into some prancing fruitcake."

Good thing Josh came shuffling out of the dressing room or Casey might have indulged in the terribly unprofessional and bad-for-business move of giving a nasty piece of her mind to a student's parent.

The boy tossed a shy half-smile at Casey. Drew Byrne showed her his back. Without so much as a nod, he pushed open the door and led his son outside.

"How obnoxious," Casey growled. But she couldn't stop herself from sneaking a peek out the window.

A gleaming white Escalade limo waited along the curb. The driver got out and held open the back door. Josh hopped inside as if he knew the drill all too well. Drew Byrne gracefully folded his large frame into the backseat next to Josh and gestured to his driver.

As the car took off, Casey suddenly remembered she had a class full of students waiting for her. She rushed back into the studio, determined not to let this arrogant jerk ruin her day any more than the tsunami of bad news that came pouring out of the letter she'd received this morning. This academy was the only thing in her life that she'd ever done right. And she wasn't about to see it go down the tubes.

~*~

They drove east through the North Fork toward the ferry. Drew gazed out the car window at the flattened runways of green earth that stretched across the horizon. Most people had no idea

Long Island's East End was so rural, a part of New York that more closely resembled New England, with farming hamlets and briny fishing villages.

For Drew Byrne, staring out at the acres of eye-settling and nerve-calming open space was as close as he ever got to being meditative. He couldn't deny there was something enchanting about the sunlight on this skinny strip of land that jutted over a hundred miles into the Atlantic.

Josh peered up at his father, his eyes wide with worry. "Dad? Did I hear you tell Miss Casey I can't go back to her school?"

"You don't need her. We can work out together at my gym. I'll get you in better shape than some ballerina can."

Josh turned away and rested his head against the window glass. Silence filled the space between them.

Drew watched his son, at first irritated. Then the dejected resignation in the slump of the boy's narrow shoulders touched his heart. What was so wrong with his idea? This always happened. Every time Drew thought things were going along pretty well, Josh would bail on him. And he never knew how to fix it.

He rested his arm over the sulky boy's shoulder. "Hey, dude, you hungry? What say we knock down some burgers?"

Josh shrugged.

"We've got the whole Fourth of July weekend together. Figured we might get a jump on the day."

The boy stared at the floor and mumbled, "Weekends begin on Friday night."

"Well, I was busy yesterday."

"You said we'd go to the new Harry Potter movie."

Damn, he'd forgotten about that. Maybe because a kid flick was hardly the way he liked spending a Friday night. At thirty-two he still preferred to chill down from an intense week of business with some female assistance. And when it came to hooking up with delicious new playthings, Drew could compete

99

with Manhattan's best.

"Maybe we'll go tonight."

"What about now? Sean saw it already."

"Sure you want to waste a beautiful sunny day inside a dark movie theater?"

"Sean said it was awesome."

"Look, we'll spend today on the boat. Fish a little. Stop at the yacht club to eat. I'll check out what's showing around Southampton tonight. And tomorrow we'll go to that horse farm where—"

"Tomorrow?" Josh sat forward. "You have to bring me back to North Cove tomorrow. For our show at the community bazaar."

"What are you talking about?"

"The Fourth of July bazaar. Mom said she told you about it."

"She did?"

Josh shook his head. "You've got too much going on, Dad. Better slow down or you'll end up with a bad stomach like Grandpa."

"Hey, I'm the father here, remember?" He gave Josh a gentle punch on the shoulder. "So what's this about?"

"Miss Casey picked me to dance in the piece she choreographed."

Drew's voice rose. "You're gonna dance in public?"

"Chill, Dad. Nobody'll see me in tights. I'll be wearing sneakers, baggy jeans, and an oversized tee. We're dancing to "Hey Ya!" by OutKast. Too cool."

"OutKast? That's hip-hop. Miss Casey does hip-hop?"

"Yeah. And she's super good at it."

"No kidding." As it was, Drew had been bothered by her sleek curves and full mouth. But the idea of Miss Prissy Ballerina getting down and dirty on the dance floor sent his X-rated imagination into overdrive.

"You won't make me miss it, Dad, will you? The other kids

are counting on me. And I don't want to let Miss Casey down."

Drew could picture that obstinate woman gloating if he allowed Josh to dance with her group tomorrow. But he could tell forbidding it would only put his already strained relationship with his son on shaky ground. And he had to admit the idea of another round of tangling with the dance teacher did have its appeal. "You like Miss Casey, huh?"

"She's great. Lots of fun. And really pretty, don't you think?"

"I guess." Who was he kidding? The little ballet teacher was downright stunning. Chestnut hair, big doe eyes. Taut, trim body. Soft and full in the just right places. When he got close to her she smelled like baby powder. And he liked how her cheeks got all pink and her juicy mouth parted as if she might—

"So can I, Dad? Come on, gangstas do hip-hop. Badass dudes."

"Watch the language, Josh."

"I get to do a flip and some B-boy moves."

"Well...okay. As long as it's none of that girly up-on-your-toes stuff."

~*~

The last of her students gone for the day, Casey stood at the desk in her waiting area rereading the awful letter from her landlord, the reality of her situation poking holes in the bravado she'd mustered this morning. A delicate piano tinkled in the background: Jiao giving a private lesson in the small studio.

Today Casey's back-to-back Saturday teaching schedule included rehearsing her Cove Corps dancers for their performance at the community bazaar. A rehearsal Josh Byrne missed. She'd gone ahead and coached a second boy in a scaled-down version of Josh's solo in case his insufferable father kept him from showing up tomorrow. The sad part was Casey saw Josh finally beginning to break out of his shyness, even letting

101

himself show off a bit in rehearsals.

When the front door opened a crack, Casey looked up to see her brother's rugged, sun-kissed face poke through. "Classes over yet?"

"All done, Parker."

With a body any Mixed Martial Arts competitor would envy and a face like Jon Hamm, Parker had as much reason as the brazen Drew Byrne to put on a macho swagger. But her tall, quiet brother seemed to have no clue how handsome he was.

He set a cardboard box on the floor. "Brought you some zucchini, tomatoes, and eggplant from my garden."

"Aha. Something tells me that last batch of ratatouille I made you wasn't all that bad."

"If you don't count the fact that even the raccoons didn't want it."

"Yeah, well, I seem to recall you ate plenty." Casey stepped around the desk and gave him a quick hug.

"You look worried."

Should she tell him? He'd always been the one she went to with her troubles. Parker had a confident, steady groundedness, which he swore came from working with trees and gardens. Casey tended to be scattered and prone to making emotional leaps onto paths leading nowhere.

She strolled across the waiting area, took a pitcher from the refrigerator, and poured iced tea into a plastic cup. "Here, bro. You look thirsty."

"That bad, huh?" Parker chugged down the tea and leaned a hip against the desk, his arms crossed over his chest. "Tell me what's up."

"Remember how I asked Mr. Vonrelis to give me at least a fifteen-year lease on this building so I could feel secure about sinking all my money into creating the academy?" Casey ran a hand through her unruly hair. "Well, he's just informed me there is a little clause in my lease that I wasn't aware of. It allows him to sell this property. And he says he's already got somebody who wants to turn this building into a restaurant."

Parker let out a slow whistle. "After all the work you put into it."

"Hey, you were a major factor in that transformation."

She shook her head thinking about how they'd cut up old Leland's Hardware Store into a small and large studio with new floors, dressing rooms with showers, lobby and office. Not to mention her apartment upstairs that would have cost her a mint to put in without a brother who knew how to do everything.

Casey flopped onto the faded green sofa and stroked tawny-colored Buster, oldest of her three cats. "None of this would have worked if you hadn't loaned me the extra money after I'd exhausted every penny of my savings. Should hang a plaque with your name on it in between my photos of Baryshnikov and Paloma Herrera."

"Sounds like you intend to fight him." Parker picked up the letter she'd left on her desk. He made a grumbling sound. "You need a lawyer to look into this."

"Know any freebies? I'm flat broke as usual."

"What about that woman on the community board?"

"No. I don't want news of this getting around. I'll lose my students. People have a way of abandoning a sinking ship. Speaking of which…" Casey put an index finger to her sealed lips as Jiao walked into the room escorting her piano student to the door.

When the student left, Jiao greeted Parker and said, "You missed some excitement here today. Your sister almost went pugilistic on a guy."

Casey groaned. Parker looked at her, eyebrows lifted in question.

Jiao laughed. "He came bursting into the middle of class and dragged his son out by the arm. Guess he couldn't get used to the idea of seeing Josh in tights."

"Who was it?" Parker asked.

"A divorced dad from out of town," Casey said, trying to

sound casual, when in fact her memory of the sexy hunk sent a rush of heat right through her. "His name's Drew Byrne."

"Drew Byrne of Byrne Trucking?"

"I don't know."

"Did you happen to notice his arms?"

Every perfectly sculpted inch of them. Casey nodded, hoping her brother didn't pick up her hormonal reaction to the man.

Parker pointed to his own shoulder. "See a tattoo of a tractor trailer on his delt?"

"I think he did have a blue truck tattooed there." Not that she could focus too well with Mr. Gorgeous standing so close.

"That's Drew," Parker said.

"You know him?"

"I work for him. He's one of my South Fork clients. He and his dad own one of the biggest trucking companies in America. Guy's filthy rich. And a powerhouse. Unlike me, plugging along to keep the business our dad started afloat, Drew Byrne turned his father's business into a Fortune 500 company."

Casey wondered if that accounted for his self-important attitude or if he'd always been that way. "Well, Mr. Powerhouse and I sort of locked horns."

She'd learned a harsh lesson in the past about guys like him. Still, a part of her was itching to ask if he'd remarried.

"Just as well," Parker said. "Byrne's a notorious womanizer. I wouldn't want him getting close enough to work his moves on my little sister."

"Not to worry," Casey said. "I steer miles away from his kind."

Note from the Author

Thanks for reading the Authors' Billboard sampler collection. If you enjoyed this first chapter of **Kiss Me, Dancer**, we hope you will consider reading the complete book and exploring the rest of the series that includes a novel featuring Casey's brother, Parker.

If you'd like to send us feedback—or just say hello—you can write us at AliciaAndRoyStreet@gmail.com We love hearing from readers and always answer every message!

About the Author

Alicia Street is a *USA Today* bestselling author. Together, Alicia and Roy are Daphne du Maurier Award-winners writing in collaboration as well as on solo projects. Roy has a background in visual arts, standup comedy and theater. Alicia spent many years as a dancer, choreographer and teacher and is a compulsive reader of every genre.

"...a husband and wife writing team that has managed to capture the best in both men's and women's fiction..."
~Romance Junkies

Contact

Visit us at –

http://aliciastreet-roystreet.com/ where you can also join our mailing list for updates and promotions!

Facebook at www.facebook.com/AliciaAndRoyStreet

Twitter – http://twitter.com/AliciaStreet1

Other books by Alicia Street

(All series books can be read as stand-alones)
DANCE 'N' LUV SERIES
Touch Me and Tango
"A very satisfying love story. Makes you want to kick up your heels and dance!"
~Romantchick
Stars, Love and Pirouettes
"Adored this book. I have read most of the Dance 'n' Luv series and enjoyed them all but this is definitely my favorite." ~Loves Reading
Snow Dance
"This book is a tender romance with real-life characters that will warm your heart and tug at your emotions." ~Rita Herron, USA Today bestselling author
Dance 'n' Luv Contemporary Romance Boxed Set
"If you've never read any of Alicia and Roy Street's romance books before, then you're in for a treat." ~Leisure Zone
Tomboy Bride
"Delightful story with a hunky H and spunky h, great storyline that keeps you on the edge of your seat." ~Something Completely Different

HOLIDAY LUV SERIES
Be Mine For Christmas
"A fabulous story. In fact, it's a story I will read over and over again." ~Amazon reader
The Christmas Honeymoon
"It is one of the best Christmas books I've read in a long time, if not forever." ~Amazon Reader
The Christmas Wedding Cake
"Loved it!" ~Amazon reader

WITH THIS RING

by

USA TODAY BEST SELLING AUTHOR

Traci Hall

Copyright © 2014 Traci Hall

Book Description

Childhood scars make it hard to trust, but true love can heal all wounds— if the lovers are willing to take the risk.

Lucia Constantine learned at an early age how to run from her emotions. Her troubled childhood forced a hard shell around her heart in order to survive. Running and hiding are cycles she's eager to break in her search for something real. As an adult, she's used therapy and art to understand her past, but has yet to commit to a relationship. Nobody has tempted her until Ronan O'Neill. The sexy bar owner comes from a family rooted deep in tradition. Trust. Love. His proposal scares her into running fast but his love just might be the anchor to keep her safe at home.

Praise

"...quick read, realistic characters and love all great qualities for an afternoon pick me up read for a romantic girl."

"...honest & open communication with each other is the most important thing in a relationship. This was a good short story with a HEA ending."

Chapter One

Lucia Constantine sat at the hundred-year-old mahogany bar, her elbow resting on the polished wood just as many a customer had before her. O'Neill's used to be a distillery in historic Savannah long before the prohibition—which remained a joke among the locals after all this time. Savannah was one of the few places where you could take your liquor in a plastic cup as you strolled beneath shady oaks, listening to the chirruping *clickety-clack* of cicadas.

Lucia didn't drink, so it made no difference to her—but her boyfriend's family had owned this same bar for that same hundred years. The O'Neills embodied Savannah's history. They were kinder than anybody she'd ever met, despite their ability to shoot whiskey as if it were water. All of them, right down to sixteen-year-old Graham–whether it was legal, or not.

She cringed when she thought of the stuff she'd done at sixteen and kept her mouth shut. Henry used to say that opinions were like assholes, and everybody had one. Didn't mean you wanted to hear from it.

"Happy birthday to you–happy birthday to you…"

She tapped her short, unpainted fingernails along the varnished wood and forced a smile as she heard thirty voices rise in celebration. Ronan O'Neill walked toward her, his dark hair a little long, but not too—he blew it back off his forehead and grinned, his exuberance sparkling like a twisting kaleidoscope. Lucia couldn't help grinning right back. She loved him, and if it made him happy to have a birthday party for her, then she'd suck it up and eat cake.

Ronan stopped before her, his turquoise eyes surrounded with dark lashes that matched his unruly curls. "Happy birthday, dear Lucia, happy birthday," he paused and did a Marilyn

Monroe impression, whispering huskily, "to. You." He held the cake in front of her. "Blow."

Her heart thumped with painful fervor, uncertain at how to react. She'd never, in all of her twenty-eight years, been so obviously cherished. Her traitorous eyes filled. "I," she started to say.

"Just blow, honey." He held the cake steady. It was shaped like a white rose in full bloom, trimmed in red chocolate-flavored frosting; designed like her logo at the tattoo shop.

She blew the candle out, leaving a tiny puff of smoke and the bar full of Ronan's relatives cheered as if she'd just scored a touchdown.

Lucia envied Ronan his childhood, growing up among people who applauded your every breath. She'd greedily absorbed the multitude of O'Neill family memorabilia hanging on the walls. Baseball games, dance recitals, church communions. Cousins and siblings and grandparents. The family she'd dreamed of having when she and her mother first hit the streets.

She'd been around five, maybe six. Those dreams of a safe, loving family had kept her believing things would be okay, until she'd realized her mother would never be well. Would never be sober, or un-addicted. Her mom chose, *always,* to get high. Lucia hadn't dreamed again until she'd learned to tattoo. A portable trade Henry had taught her, where all she needed was her kit, stocked with needles and ink.

"Here," Ronan said, handing her a wrapped package.

"No gifts." Lucia's cheeks flamed. "You promised, Ronan." The last thing she wanted was a bunch of presents. She never liked owing anybody.

"Just a small one." He nodded at his father, who stood at the bar. A tray of champagne flutes were handed around, though Lucia barely noticed, ensnared in the love blazing from Ronan's eyes. *For me.*

He leaned forward with a kiss. One of the most amazing

things about Ronan was his wealth of compassion. She rarely had to explain her feelings; he seemed to understand that they sometimes weighed heavy. "You are the best gift I could ask for," she whispered against his lips. "I don't need anything but you."

"I feel the same way." He took her hand and brushed his mouth lightly across her knuckles.

Absorbing his words, her heart unfurled like a budded flower coaxed alive by the sun. Ronan dared her to believe in fairy tales, even though she knew better.

He accepted a glass of champagne and passed a flute of club soda with lime to Lucia. He'd been respectful of her story, the parts she'd shared—which were cleaned up versions of the truth.

His brother Jaime, red-haired like their father, clapped his hand on Ronan's shoulder and laid a resounding smack of his lips against Lucia's cheek. "Happy birthday, Lucia. I still can't believe you picked the brother too chicken for a tattoo."

Ronan's blue eyes flashed and Lucia laughed.

"He got a tattoo." She smiled at the memory. "You boys had a few too many after Matthew's bachelor party..."

Matthew hooted from the back, raising his new wife Moira's hand, her diamond ring catching the light.

"Sorry, Lucia," Moira called.

With a dismissive wave, Lucia said, "No, no. It was my lucky day. Four handsome men stumbling into the tattoo parlor, all wanting a souvenir."

Banter and jokes went around the bar and Ronan's mother, a porcelain-skinned woman with dark hair, shook her head in mock shame—though Lucia had spent the last six months realizing that nothing Patricia O'Neill's boys did would ever lose her love.

Mother's love was supposed to be unconditional, but this was the first Lucia had seen of it. She held onto to the thread of the story, refusing to give her past any more power.

"And who falls into my chair, but this one?" She ruffled

111

Ronan's hair, the silly gesture fueling her feelings for him. Even drunk, he'd treated her with respect, careful of her things, calling her ma'am.

"He needed a tattoo, by the most beautiful tattoo artist in Savannah," Jaime said. "You'd just moved here, and already built a reputation."

"I'd never heard of you before," Ronan confessed.

"You never had a tattoo before!" Matthew shouted from the back.

"Too chicken." Jaime lifted his glass in salute. "Which was my point."

Lucia sighed expressively. "And how could I turn him down, when he asked for my best work with such sincerity?"

Ronan, taking the jibes in stride, went with the teasing which was part of being an O'Neill. "I sprawled out before her, a sacrifice on her altar-"

"No poetry," teenaged Graham yelled.

"His poetry sings, baby brother." Shannon, the youngest daughter at twenty-two, punched Graham in the arm. "Just because you learned to rhyme with Dr. Seuss doesn't mean one of our clan can't have some class."

"I love your poetry," Lucia said, stealing a kiss from Ronan's mouth. "And I did as you asked. I gave you a tattoo to be proud of."

Jaime leaned over, laughing so hard his face turned red. "I Love Mom." He looked toward their mother. "No offense, Ma."

Patricia rolled her eyes.

"It was a fine tattoo." Lucia's lips twitched. "And you were happy enough with it when you went home that night. But the next morning?" She shuddered. "Showing up at the parlor in a rage." Lucia smoothed her hand over Ronan's bicep. "You were furious. Adorable, but angry."

"You laughed when I told you I would sue you." Ronan slid his arm around her waist.

"Sue her?" Patricia asked with disbelief. "It was your drunk ass that got the tattoo!"

"I know, Ma. I'm not proud, but imagine my surprise, waking up that morning with a head ache and a giant heart on my arm." Ronan stood next to Lucia and played to the crowd. "I threatened her with everything I could think of. She finally licked her finger and swiped it through the ink. It smudged."

His mother gave a startled laugh. "Serves you right, Ronan. Poor Lucia. I'm shocked she agreed to date you at all."

"I realized I'd been a jerk and I begged her to let me apologize with breakfast." Ronan kissed her cheek.

Lucia leaned so that they were arm to arm as they faced his relatives. "He was very smooth over bacon and toast. And when he poured maple syrup over his eggs?" Lucia shrugged. It was her favorite way to eat them, but not for the faint of heart. "I had to give him a chance."

Ronan held up his hand for quiet as his family laughed. "You've stalled long enough. Open your gift."

Lucia, smiling as she recalled the expression on his face as he'd realized his tattoo was fake, pulled the ribbon free from a pretty silver box. She lifted the lid, then stared at Ronan with confusion. "What?"

He faltered as he saw her reaction, then brazened through. "Lucia Constantine, I fell in love with you that day. Will you marry me?"

Responses whizzed furiously through Lucia's brain. She'd made her opinions on marriage clear—bondage, with no escape route for either party. Not even children were a reason to tie the knot.

Hadn't he known she was serious?

He stared at her with love and dawning realization. She blinked quickly before she gave anything else away.

She loved this man as she'd loved no other. She trusted him, and adored his family. They all stared at her with expectant smiles.

Sick to her stomach, she thrust the ring into his hands.

"No."

~*~

Ronan watched in what amounted to shock as Lucia ran from the bar. Her dark curls flowed behind her, her floral print dress with the red tulle skirt and candy apple high heels rounded the corner before he could think to go after her.

He turned to his family, who all stared at him, stunned.

Finally Shannon said, "That *bitch.*"

Liam O'Neill gave his daughter a reproving look. "None of that," he boomed. "Come, Ronan. Talk to me in the back." Liam gestured toward the office behind the bar, his dad getting him out of the spot light as he tried to understand what just happened.

He'd just offered his heart, for the first time in his life, to the woman he knew down to his toes was the one meant for him.

She'd humiliated him by turning him down.

In all of the scenarios running through his head, he'd never imagined that.

~*~

Ronan faced his father across the desk piled high with old receipts, pictures and an ancient calculator that still ran on an AA battery.

"Well," his dad said with a gruff voice. "That was unexpected."

Wincing, Ronan gave a curt nod as he sat back in the wooden chair. "Yeah."

"You wouldn't a put her on the spot, if you'd been figuring a yes." Liam's thick fingers drummed against the papers on the desk, his expression neutral as he watched Ronan.

"She doesn't like to be the center of attention," Ronan admitted with a helpless shrug. *Was that why she said no?* "But she loves me. I love her. We're moving in together." They'd

114

talked about it last month. They just had to wait until her lease was up.

"I believe that she loves you—I've seen it. But how well do you really know her, son? Six months of dating isn't that long." His dad picked up a small framed picture of his wife, taken in the late seventies. His mom looked like a hippie chick, complete with a flower in her dark hair.

"You asked Mom to marry you the day you met."

His dad nodded, his mouth set. "Luckiest day of my life." Liam kissed the picture and returned it to the mess.

"I mean," Ronan pressed, knowing he couldn't be wrong. "You *knew*."

"O'Neills are lucky that way. Never heard of a one that won the lottery, but finding love, that we got."

Ronan rubbed at his aching heart, replaying the flare of Lucia's skirt as she ran out of the bar. Away from him. "We love each other."

"As wonderful as that feels, sometimes love isn't enough to make a life." His dad hesitated. "She never really talks about her past. Maybe there's a reason for that?"

"She's a private person, Dad." Ronan knew she'd been hurt, badly. Her mother's addictions, her dad's abandonment. She didn't like to talk about it—preferred to act as if her childhood hadn't happened. She seemed well-adjusted, so he hadn't pried. He guessed she'd grown up with her grandma.

"We've noticed she doesn't drink," Liam said in a voice that withheld judgment. "Is she an alcoholic? That might scare a woman, getting hitched to a bar owner if she's got a jones for the punch."

"Not her." Ronan sighed, wondering if the bar was too big a bad memory and Lucia just didn't want to tell him. Because he knew his dad cared, he shared some of what he Lucia had told him. "Her mother was the addict. Not just booze."

"Is that why she's moved around so much?" Liam sat back, lacing his fingers behind his head. "Listening to her talk about her travels is interesting, Ronan, but not the sign of a woman thinking to settle down."

"It isn't her fault she went from place to place!" Ronan realized he spoke defensively and lowered his voice. "She went where her mother took them."

"As a child yes, but she's all grown now." His dad coughed into his fist, his discomfort obvious at saying things that might hurt him. "Every few months she packs up and moves. Why, son?"

Ronan didn't have an answer. He'd assumed she'd stay put once she found love. Stability. A normal life. Was he off-base?

"I'm not telling you what to do, but Lucia is no stray puppy you can bring home and nurse to health. Marriage is a commitment between two like-minded adults. You can't marry someone who's broken and expect to have a healthy relationship."

"Dad." Ronan's simmering anger grew in defense of the woman he loved. How had today gone so wrong? "She's not damaged goods, for Christ's sake."

Liam held up his hand. "You have a great heart, Ronan, always have. It's what makes you so good with your poetry, and a wonder behind the bar. You feel, you care, and people respond to that. But you can't fix every wounded soul that crosses your path."

"She doesn't need fixing! Lucia is fiercely independent, but she's had to be in order to survive. So what if she doesn't want to get married?" As he said the words, disappointment fell like volcanic ash. He'd wanted the white picket fence since he'd understood what it meant.

His dad's thick red brows hiked upward. "It's how we do it, son. Marriage, kids. We O'Neills have had this bar for a hundred years, getting married and raising our families right here. It's tradition."

Did his dad see something in Lucia that Ronan had missed? Was she really so messed up? He'd admired her edgy humor.

Spent hours trying to understand her prickly need to do things for herself—he'd had to win a round of poker just to open the door for her without resistance.

Damn. Had he been pushing her to fit into his world?

He shouldn't have pressured her, in front of everyone. Hell, to be honest, she'd gotten spooked when he'd brought up living together. He sank down in the chair, realizing he hadn't been considerate of *her* feelings at all.

"There are many kinds of love." His dad shrugged, concern in his eyes. "I suggest taking a few days and cooling off. Examine what you really feel for Lucia. Just maybe she did you a favor. I don't want to see you miserable ten years down the road, Ronan." He jabbed his pointer finger against the desk. "Sometimes a woman is too broken to mend."

"You don't know her." Ronan got to his feet, his body overwhelmed with a rush of adrenalin. His arms and legs shook as if he'd run five miles in an all-out sprint. All he could think about was making this right.

"Do you?" His dad crossed his arms over his chest, refusing to look away.

"I made a mistake, putting her on the spot." Ronan rubbed two fingers between his brows, pressing against the building ache. "I did what I wanted, thinking she'd want it too. I was wrong. But, Dad, that doesn't mean I'm giving up on her." Ronan held his dad's sympathetic gaze, wanting him to understand. "She's the strongest woman I've ever known. I didn't consider her past—and I should have. I handled my proposal all wrong."

"Ronan, wait a day or two. Emotions are high," Liam cautioned.

"Emotions? *Passion.* Love." Ronan unclenched his fists. "I wouldn't have it any other way."

He should have realized from the beginning that Lucia opening her heart to him was something fragile between them. Instead of nurturing the love they'd grown he'd shoved it in the

chaos of his life—wanting her to thrive in it because he did.
And that was just my first mistake.

A Note from the Author

If you enjoyed this first chapter from With This Ring (a short story series) you can find the rest of the book at Amazon: Please recommend and review the book.

About the Author

With an impressive bibliography in an array of genres, USA Today bestselling author Traci Hall has garnered a notable fan base. She pens stories guaranteed to touch the heart while transporting the reader to another time and place. Her belief in happily ever after shines through, whether it's a romantic glimpse into history or a love affair for today.

Contact

Website: http://tracihall.com
Facebook: http://facebook.com/traciella
Pinterest: https://www.pinterest.com/tracihallauthor/

Other books by Traci Hall

Other books in this short story series:

Always a Bridesmaid
Never a Bride

Other Contemporary Romance novels, By the Sea series:

Ambrosia by the Sea
Karma by the Sea
Puppy Love by the Sea

Historical Romance, western series:

Crimson Gold
Silver Sky
Medieval Romance series:
The Queen's Guard: Rose (Violet and Peony)

THE SMARTEST HORSE IN TEXAS

The Traherns, Western Pioneer series

by

Nancy Radke

Copyright © 2013 Nancy Radke

Book Description

He rode a stolen horse into Texas.

Honor demanded Matthew return the horse he stole before he married the lady he loved.

Praise:

"If you like horses you really will enjoy this book. It's humorous, serious, sad, funny, interesting and well written. It teaches good moral lessons, shows how racially prejudice some people are, and how easily we can hurt people. Really good book. Also good book about how to treat animals. Not a mushy romance but is a love story."

~ Phycilla

"I thoroughly enjoyed this book. The characters were real, including the horse, Hero. The descriptive writing drew me in like a living experience. I use to own and train horses so I appreciated the horse sense running through the story as well as a sweet romance."

~ Donia

Chapter One

A man should never have to ride bareback on a bony horse. At least not very far. It 'bout cuts him in two.

I wouldn't have been riding this way, except some sneak thief stole my mount, saddle and all, and took off, leaving me this bag of bones. I'm a big man and at least the "bones" had long enough legs that my feet didn't trail in the dirt, but I did have to watch out when we passed rocks and thorn bushes. That was about all the good I could say about him.

The horse stolen from me, named Hero, was a heap better. I would a been right put out, except I stole Hero in the first place, during the war, and it didn't seem quite right to make a fuss over a horse that wasn't mine. But Hero was a powerful stallion and more horse than most men ever get a chance to ride, and I missed him. I aimed to get him back.

When the war was over, I rode Hero back to my old home. My ma and pa were still alive and I spent a year there, helping them rebuild and get some crops in. The next spring, I left to make my own way. Their farm could only sustain two people at the most. I rode south through Ft. Smith and down the Butterfield Trail, headed toward El Paso. I figured to find me a place in Texas and build a ranch.

According to my cousin, Trey, there were thousands of longhorn cows running through the Texas brush, breeding like jackrabbits, just waiting for a rope to be dropped on them. He'd put together a herd and brought it up to Independence, Missouri, just after the war broke out. A man with a loop and a running iron could soon have himself a large herd. A few trips north would give a poor man a big stake in a short time.

I'd swapped my tattered Rebel uniform for some clothes at a small Cherokee Indian village. They were delighted with the brass buttons and the colonel's three stars on the collar. I couldn't be shut of that uniform fast enough, and was happy they wanted it. Many of their tribe had fought with the Confederates, and they were facing an uncertain future.

Of course they wanted Hero, but he and I had gone

123

through the last weeks of the war together. No one got him. At least, he wasn't for sale.

The pants I'd traded for looked like they'd last a spell, made of heavy cord cloth. I now had a buckskin shirt, and, the best trade of the lot, a sturdy pair of high-topped moccasins which one of the women had made for me there on the spot. Riding boots were made for riding, and I needed to be able to rest my feet now and then. Unlike many horsemen, I liked to walk, but just not in boots.

They thought my red underwear and my worn out army blanket would be perfect, woven into a blanket. I got one of their heavy blankets in exchange for them. I had brought in a fat buck I'd shot, and we all shared the meat. As I left, they offered me some pemmican, and I happily accepted, storing the dried meat in my saddlebags.

I had just crossed a dry stretch of prairie when my fortunes reversed.

Finding a tiny stream that barely had a trickle flowing, I had dismounted to get a drink. I'd loosened my cinch so Hero could rest while I gathered an armload of rocks to dam up the creek and give him a good drink. It had been done before, so I just had to round up the rocks and put them back in their places.

That there thief must have been lying in the brushy rocks all along, for Hero didn't even raise his head until the gent stood up and demanded I hand him over.

I had my arms full of rocks and my gun in its holster, tied down. He had a gun in his hand. He swung aboard and took off and I stood there watching to see if my loose cinch would spin the saddle on him. It didn't. I could have tried to shoot him off of Hero, but I valued that horse too much.

Also, being a stallion, he just might be too much horse for a thief.

I put my rocks in the stream, waited a minute, then got a good drink and looked around for something to carry water in. I didn't have any illusions about trying to cross that desert stretch up ahead without a way to carry water and my empty canteen had gone north with that thief. He hadn't even taken the time to fill it, making me wonder if he had any bullets in his gun. Well, he now had my Henry rifle and extra ammo in the saddlebags.

A soft nicker alerted me.

124

It had come from behind a large rocky outcrop, and I walked carefully around to the other side. There lay this thin white horse, half-dead. I ran back and filled my hat with water and carried it up to him. I washed out his mouth and got him to drink a few swallows. Then some more.

I refilled my hat, then helped him drink, cupping the water into his mouth.

So this was how that gent had got here. He probably thought his horse was dead and looked upon my arrival as an early Christmas. If he'd have known he was stealing a horse from a Trahern, he might have reconsidered first.

Our family had no quit in them. Men or women, once we set our minds on a thing, we didn't stop, even if it took years. My cousin, Trey, was as likely as not hunting me down right now. I needed to have Hero to give back to him. Trey wouldn't take it kindly if I lost his horse.

The thief's outfit was also there, an empty tin canteen and an old Sharps rifle with no bullets. The horse had a bridle, but no saddle.

I took that white horse to water and watched as he got himself a drink and then another one. Then he flopped down on the dirt with a groan and rested.

I checked his feet. He had one shoe off and another just hanging, so I worked it off with my knife. Then I got another drink and filled the canteen left by the thief. I screwed down the cap and put it to soak in the stream, so the wet cloth covering would keep the water inside cool.

Then I took me a drink a little upstream, then another, and finally got that horse up and gave him one more deep drink before we started out.

That thief had been mighty dumb, for he had taken Hero just as I'd completed a long waterless trek, and he hadn't bothered to let him get a drink. He also wasn't riding with any water, because I'd run out before I reached the stream. I hoped I would find him before Hero was killed. I'd taken a liking to that stallion, ever since I had lifted him from Trey, who was fighting on the Union side.

I'd always ridden carefully and my mounts were always in good shape. I think the white horse must have appreciated the rest and the water, for he started out at a fast trot, and it nigh bounced the insides out of me. He had the roughest trot I'd every tried to sit, and with no stirrups, I couldn't hold myself away from his boney withers unless I held myself back with my hands or pulled my knees high.

I settled him down into a fast walk and decided he must have some Walker in him, because his gait smoothed out and he walked faster than his trot.

I scooted myself back a mite towards his rump and let him go, following Hero's trail, which was headed north. Not the direction I had been traveling, but I was determined to get Hero back.

Towards evening, the white started slowing down. I slid off and walked a bit to let him rest. I'd been walking now and then, and my feet were so sore from my high-heeled boots, I could hardly stand. I made an early dry camp in a stand of cacti. I drank from the canteen and gave the white a sip of water from a stem of cactus. It didn't work all that well, but it did have some water in it. I slept for a few hours while the sand was warm. It got cold, but the moon came out, lighting up the trail and I led that horse out and we walked a good many miles before the sun came up.

Later that morning we were taking another rest when a group of five riders descended upon us, rifles at the ready and looking for bear.

"That's his horse," one of the men cried out, spurring his horse to plunge down the slope to where I stood.

I lifted my hands, for they looked to be ready to shoot on sight, and I didn't want any bullets flying my way.

One youngster shook out a rope and that I really didn't want to see, although there were no trees nearby. *So I was going to get hung as a horse thief after all, for a horse I hadn't stolen.*

Well, I'd give it a good talk. "Before you gents get all worked up, why don't you take the time to check out some facts."

The youngster glared at me. "We don't listen to no lyin' murderin'—"

Murder was it? So he had been more than a horse thief. "Even if I told you my horse was stolen from me by the man who almost rode this one to death."

"How come you're alive, then?" he said with a sneer,

making his loop.

"Cause I don't think he had any bullets in his gun when he grabbed my horse. I didn't realize it until he rode away. I had dismounted at that small stream back up the trail a ways, and he snuck out of the bushes and took off on my horse. He's a sorrel stallion with three white stockings and half a star. My name's on the saddle. It's a Texas double-rigged. I intend to get my outfit back—so if you folks have cause to want part of his hide, you can stand in line."

I started to put my hands down, then saw they weren't accepting me yet. One of them dismounted and took my pistol and the old Sharps rifle. "This is Joe's rifle, James. Got his name carved into the stock."

"What's your name?" the oldest man demanded. He looked to be the one in charge, so I spoke to him.

"Matthew Trahern."

"Trahern? I've heard of you. Out of Ohio."

"Not me. But I've plenty of kin, so it could easily be a brother or cousin. I've come up from Arkansas. What did the man do, who took my horse?"

"Killed my brother. That's his horse you've got."

"Well, if you hang me, you're not going to get justice. I can prove where I was the last week or so. When did this happen?"

"Two days ago."

"Well, six days ago I was at Fort Smith. Having dinner with Major Grannon and his wife."

"His knees are bad, Uncle Jim," the youngster said, pointing to the white horse.

"He's been ridden to the ground," I said. "But he's got a stout heart, even if his back is all bone."

"His name's Jack," one man said.

"He got some Tennessee Walker in him, I think," I said to him. "Even with sore feet, he sure can cover the ground."

"Put that rope away," the older man told the youngster. "I'm James Cummings. You come with us while we get this straightened out."

The youngster scowled, but coiled up the rope, letting me breathe easier.

"Any of you men read sign?" I asked.

"I do," Cummings said.

"Then lookee here. See that track? That's my horse. His back shoe has a notch in it. He's big, purt near eighteen hands. You can see how far apart the tracks are. You'll be able to spot him right off. I need my horse and gear so I can find work, so I'm following that trail."

The kid spoke again. "What if we don't believe—"

"Quiet." Cummings cut the youngster off. "We'll follow it. It's mighty fresh."

"I've been gaining on him. He doesn't know how to ride this country and save his horse." *Neither did they, for their horses were all lathered and breathing hard. Horses were cheap compared to most things, but a good horse had a value that couldn't be figured in money.*

I gave Jack another drink out of my canteen and I think that sealed my case for Cummings.

He nodded and relaxed, then waited for me to jump on and we rode off, following the track of the killer. I traveled as fast as possible, for I could see Hero was getting in a bad way, staggering from lack of water.

Cummings could see it too. "He'll kill your horse," he said. He turned toward the youngster.

"George, get down."

"What? Why?"

"Give your horse to Mr. Trahern here. You follow us slow on your pa's horse. We're going to hurry and catch this man before he gets away."

"Thanks," I said, swinging my foot over the white horse's neck and stepping to the ground.

The youngster glared at me as he got off and handed me his reins. I ignored him, knowing he was still too young to have much sense, and gave him the reins to his father's horse. I didn't offer to boost him on. There were plenty of boulders around if he needed help mounting.

Around noon, we came over a rise and there stood Hero, in the shade of a yucca tree. We stopped and scattered back into cover behind some rocks.

Hero walked down the trail and right up to me. He still had my saddle on and I noticed that the thief had cinched it too tight. The man had also used his spurs on him. I could see the bloody marks.

Now I didn't wear spurs when riding Hero for a reason. He never took too kindly to them.

"Mr. Cummings, I think my horse dumped your killer up the trail a ways. My rifle is here, which means he's probably unarmed. And, I think...yes, here's the money." I untied a bag and handed it to him.

That murderer had tore up Hero's mouth yanking on the bit. I took off the bridle and put on his halter. Then I took off my hat, opened my canteen and poured Hero a drink in it. He drank it all, sucking up the last moisture, and I marveled that he was still standing.

"You gave all your water to your horse?" one of the younger riders said, making it sound like some strange thing.

"If he don't make it, I don't make it."

I pulled my moccasins from behind the cantle, took off my boots and switched footwear. My feet were mighty happy to have those moccasins on.

James Cummings had been watching, and I called him closer and pulled back my saddlebags so he could see the back of the cantle.

"In case there's any doubt," I said, "here's my name on my saddle." It was branded in, my cousin had done it with the tip of a running iron. Trahern

Nothin' fancy, but it marked that outfit as mine. Or so they thought.

He looked and nodded.

"Give him back his gun, Brandy."

I walked over and got my pistol back. With the rifle in the scabbard and my pistol in my holster, I felt ready for battle again. I opened my saddlebags to check my ammunition. That thief had rummaged around in them, making a mess, but all my bullets were there.

"We should go find your killer while he's still trying to recover from what Hero did to him," I said. "He didn't take any of my bullets, so they must not fit his gun."

They mounted up and rode along the trail, single file, with me bringing up the rear, leading Hero, who walked with a limp. About a half mile along, Hero stopped, snorted, his head and tail high, nostrils flared, at full alert. He spun and looked at an area in the brush, quivering.

This time I had my pistol in my hand. I looked down to where Hero's tracks came out of the brush. They were next to a long broken track in the dust showing the passage of a sidewinder, a rattlesnake that travels sideways to go forward. Instead of charging straight into the battle, I'd do like that sidewinder and sort of sidle up to it, checking things out as I went.

I dropped Hero's reins and slipped around through the bushes, making sure I kept some cover between me and the killer.

It was him all right. He was pretty beat up. I think Hero might have stepped on him a bit after he threw him off, just to teach him a few things about handling a stallion. And I had guessed right. He had no bullets in his gun. He didn't even try for it.

"Cummings! Here's your man."

Cummings and his men rode up and dismounted.

"That's the man you want," the thief yelled, pointing at me. "He stole my horse."

A Note from the Author

If you enjoyed this first chapter from THE SMARTEST HORSE IN TEXAS, (The Traherns, Western Pioneer series,) you can find the whole book on various platforms. Please recommend and review the book.

About the Author

An Amazon top 100 author, Nancy Radke grew up on a wheat and cattle ranch, and her western background shows in the Trahern series, which is currently at 13 books. Her narrative writing is often compared with Louis L'Amour's westerns (the voice, not the plots). She keeps her books free of heavy sexual scenes and swearing

Contact

http://www.nancyradkeauthor.com
https://www.facebook.com/AuthorNancyRadke
https://www.facebook.com/nancy.radke.336
https://www.pinterest.com/bible4children/
https:// google.com/+Nancyradkeauthorteacher

Other books by Nancy Radke

The Traherns: 3 collections #1, #2, #3.
Sisters of Spirit: 2 collections
The Handsomest Man in the Country, The Traherns #1
The Prettiest Girl in the Land, The Traherns #3
The Luckiest Man in the West, The Traherns #4
The Happiest Man in the Territory, The Traherns #5
The Stubbornest Girl in the Valley, The Traherns #6
The Tallest Man in Texas, The Traherns #7
The Quietest Woman in the South, The Traherns #8
The Bravest Woman in the Town, The Traherns #9
The Richest Man in Texas, The Traherns #10
The Loneliest Man in the Mountains, The Traherns #11
The Toughest Man in the Territory, The Traherns #12
The Sunniest Gal from Tennessee, The Traherns #13
Height of Danger, Brothers of Spirit #1
Turnagain Love, Sisters of Spirit #1
Closed Doors, Sisters of Spirit #2
Stolen Secrets, Sisters of Spirit #3
Courage Dares, Sisters of Spirit #4
Songs for Perri, Sisters of Spirit #5
Tennessee Touch, Sisters of Spirit #6
Spirit of a Champion, Sisters of Spirit #7
Appaloosa Blues, Sisters of Spirit #8
A Tennessee Christmas (short novella includes Sisters of
Spirit characters)

Watch for The Trahern Audio books as they are released.

MUCH ADO ABOUT MINERS

Hearts of Owyhee Series

by

AWARD WINNING AUTHOR

Jacquie Rogers

Which is more likely to be stolen—the silver, or his heart?

Copyright © 2013 Jacquie Rogers

Book Description

Cupid's bullet...

Hired gun Kade McKinnon interrupts a bank holdup and is shot by the teller, Iris Gardner, whose victims have a tendency to be the next groom in town. Will he be the groom this time?

Cupid's bow...

Iris Gardner, a smart, independent bank clerk, fell in love with Kade when she was too young to know better. So when he walks back into her life and her bank, it's only fitting that she shoots him ... by accident, of course.

Cupid's blindfold...

Kade doesn't know Iris's company is the one who hired him to escort a bullion shipment, and Iris doesn't know Kade owns the security company, but they both know robbers are on their trail. Which is more likely to be stolen--the silver, or his heart?

Praise

"Rogers' delightful characters bring their own distinct flavor to **Much Ado About Miners***: the Shakespeare quoting sidekick.. This entertaining tale will have you rooting for the good guys while hanging on for a wild and fun ride that starts on the first page and doesn't let up to the very end."*

~ Chanticleer Book Reviews

*"**Much Ado About Miners** rocks the cowboy world! Sexy gunman Kade, groom-shooting bank clerk Iris, and a warrior cat will keep you in stitches and warm your heart at the same time. I love this series!"*

~BookwormForever

Chapter One

Iris Gets Her Man

July, 1885—Silver City, Idaho Territory

Iris Gardner rubbed her eyes, then put her spectacles back on and resumed summing the never-ending columns of numbers in the bank's ledgers. A plunge in a cool stream would be heavenly on such a sweltering hot day, but here she was, stuck in the stuffy teller's cage until five o'clock.

Much as she enjoyed keeping the books for Hewett and Sons Bank, and she truly did, the patronizing Mr. Hewett was a perfect example of an egotistical male who didn't think women were good for anything except cleaning and breeding. She'd show him. Suffragists can meet any challenge!

In just three weeks, she'd never have to put up with a man again.

The manager scooted his chair back from his desk and stood a moment, stretching his rheumatiz back, then donned his derby. "I have a meeting but I'll be back before closing." He tapped the counter in front of her with his cane as he passed.

She smiled and nodded. His meeting was probably at the Silver Slipper and involved a bottle of Owyhee County's finest spirits, a Havana cigar, and a deck of cards. Iris didn't care. She'd balance the books far more quickly without him. She could also check his mining investments—following them had given her quite an education, which she'd used to her advantage.

He paused in front of the teller's cage. "Are you ready for the masquerade ball a week from Saturday?"

"Yes, sir."

"Good. Maybe we can get you a husband." The banker

135

twirled his cane and left.

Mr. Hewett meant his son, Edward. Iris had no intention of marrying the younger Mr. Hewett, or any other man. The only man she wanted didn't want her, so the next best option was to make her own way. An independent woman didn't require a husband for either prosperity or propriety. Nevertheless, she loved dancing and looked forward to the ball.

The social scene in Silver City had been lacking the past few years, making the masquerade ball the talk of the town. Iris smiled just thinking about it. Fairies loved to dance as did she, and she'd spent months planning and sewing. She'd go as Titania, Queen of the Fairies from *A Midsummer Night's Dream*. The play had been a favorite of her and her friends when the Gardner family had lived in Virginia City, Nevada, so long ago, and Titania was, of course, her favorite of all characters.

Now that her oldest and best friend, Vivvie McKinnon, had moved to the area, they'd rekindled both their friendship and their love of the theater. More important, Vivvie had invested in the Bonnet Consortium, a mining investment company, with Iris and three other ladies.

Just as Iris had added halfway down the credits column, jangling spurs and clomping boots in the lobby distracted her.

"Stay right there, little lady. Don't move."

Iris's mouth went dry and her insides turned to jelly. Four dusty, ragged bandits, dirty bandanas covering their faces up to their beady eyes, crouched ready for action with their six-guns pointed right at her. They were too far away for her to see them well with her spectacles on, but she had no doubt they meant business of the dangerous sort. She swallowed hard and tried to calm herself but staring down four pistol barrels convinced her she could die fighting or she could die standing there.

"Damn, Scud, a lady banker. Never seen one of them before!"

"A banker's a banker." He cocked the pistol and Iris knew they planned to kill her—either with a bullet or their rank odor.

The outlaw closest to her added, "And the only good banker is a dead banker."

They left her no choice. If she ever wanted to be an independent woman of means, if she ever wanted to wear that fairy costume, she had to fend for herself.

"Open the safe."

Mr. Hewett had never given her the combination, but she nodded to buy some time and concentrate on keeping her heart from slamming into her throat. If she had to die, at least one of them would have to give his life for it. Slowly, cautiously, she moved her hand under the counter, taking care that her shoulder didn't give away the movement. Feeling for the Peacemaker next to the till, she waited for her opportunity.

"Don't just stand there, woman. Open the safe!"

"Yes, sir," she whispered, her voice quivering, then raised the pistol, fired twice in their general direction. The pistol's recoil forced her arms up and her right arm sent her spectacles flying but she couldn't worry about that, because the lobby chandelier shattered.

"Get down!" the leader ordered amidst the yelping. A couple of them ended up with cuts from the flying glass shards. Her shots hadn't exactly gone where she wanted them, but that last one had been effective.

She ducked behind the solid oak counter with the hope it would shield her from return fire. A couple of deep breaths calmed her shaky nerves. The bandits hadn't left yet, but they would. No one who messed with Iris Gardner would leave without a lesson in politeness. She pointed her pistol through the cage and, not even looking, she fired twice more.

One man cried out and she heard a *thunk*. A lucky shot.

"Bone's hurt!" one of them yelled.

Another hollered, "Let's get out of here before the law comes."

Iris stood as three men retreated, dragging the fourth man, and she fired off another round just to make good and sure they didn't change their minds. A fifth man went down. Only this man was also shooting at the bandits.

Her heart thumped and she didn't know whether to hide, run for help, or throw up.

The bandits hightailed it down Jordan Street, leaving a trail of dust. Iris hurried to the fifth man who lay still, blood pooling at the side of his head and soaking into the boardwalk. "Oh, please don't let him be dead," she whispered as she knelt beside him.

The man was quite nicely formed. She couldn't see his face because his hat covered it, and with her spectacles somewhere on the floor of the teller's cage, focusing was out of the question. Unfortunately, she was extremely far-sighted and although she could see objects across the room or farther way, anything closer was a blur.

And anyway, she wasn't sure she wanted to see the face of the man she'd shot. Her throat tightened and she was sick with remorse.

By then, several people had crowded around her, and Sheriff Sidney Adler pushed his way through. He squatted by the stranger.

"Does he have a pulse?"

"I... I didn't touch him."

Sheriff Adler pressed his forefinger to the side of the prone man's neck. "Strong heartbeat. Anyone call Doc Mabry yet?" He nodded at the grocer. "Have him meet us at my office. I'll need four men to carry this big fellow to the jail." The sheriff examined the head wound. "Looks like just a scratch. Hope so— head wounds can be nasty." He leaned back on his haunches. "Miss Gardner, did you shoot this man?"

"Yes, sir."

"Attempted bank robbery?"

"Yes, but—"

He cut her off before she could tell him this man wasn't one of the robbers. "Did they take any money or valuables?"

"No, but—"

"How many others were there?"

"Four, but—"

"Which way did they ride out?"

"South, but—"

He flipped a coin to a boy. "Go get my deputy." Then he turned to Iris. "Are you unhurt, Miss Gardner?"

"Yes, but—"

"Come to my office so I can make a report and press charges." He stood and motioned for the men still there to pick up the fallen man.

"But, Sheriff—"

* * *

Kade McKinnon woke to ringing in his ears and a twenty-mule team dancing the polka on his skull. He had no doubt that if he opened his eyes, hot pokers would slash through his brain. Best to concentrate on steady breathing until he could figure out where the blazes he was and what sort of trouble he was in. This time.

Only he wasn't alone. The sweet smell of a lady filled the musty room, and her footfalls and swishing skirts indicated pacing back and forth. A troubled lady. He wanted to take a look-see but the bass drum pounding in his head assuaged his curiosity.

"How is he, Doc?" The voice came from a worried woman.

"He'll wake up with a headache, but he's none the worse for the wear as far as I can see."

"Good. I didn't mean to shoot him."

"You marrying this one?"

"Doc!" The woman sounded truly upset. Hell, he wasn't that bad looking. Of course, he wasn't the marrying type, either.

"I'll be on my way—have another call to make. Let me know if he vomits or has a seizure." Footfalls sounded and then Kade heard the door open and shut.

"Sheriff, at least tell me what I'm charged with."

Sheriff? Damn, he must be in jail. The woman's voice was not angry, as Kade would've expected, but more resigned, and he didn't doubt she truly was sorry for shooting him.

"Nothing yet, Miss Gardner. I'll take your statement when all the ruckus dies down, but for now, I don't want you talking about the case."

Miss Gardner? That name was familiar—not recently familiar—something Kade had known for years. But Gardner was a common name and he dismissed the thought, mostly because it hurt too much to think.

"Then why am I here?"

"I want you here. Once I get the facts straight, I'll talk to Judge Glover and we'll make a decision."

"But Sidney, I can tell you what happened."

Miss Gardner's on a first-name basis with the sheriff?

"Once this fellow wakes up, we'll do that. Meantime, I've sent a message to your mother—good thing she's in town—to bring a change of clothes. Wilfred's heating up some water now."

"Do you know his name?" Miss Gardner asked. "He's familiar but I'm sure he doesn't have an account at the bank."

"We'll find out when he regains consciousness. Probably just a drifter."

"Silver City is an out-of-the-way place to drift."

Kade thought it best to remain still. He needed time to think, and things weren't working too good upstairs. Where the hell was Phineas? Virgin Alley, more than likely. His partner was getting up in the years, but any time they rode into a town, the old prospector wasted no time finding the company of a soiled dove.

Another woman entered the sheriff's office. He knew it was a woman because of the whish of her skirts.

"Iris Gardner, what have you done?" A stern, matronly voice.

Iris Gardner. He'd known a girl with that name—his little

140

sister's best friend when they lived in Virginia City. The Gardner family had moved away years ago, before he'd left home.

"My job, Mama."

"Your job does not include shooting men. The last one you shot married your sister." Kade heard her walk closer. "And this one's even better looking."

The last one?

"You'll never let me live that down, will you?"

"Probably not." Keys jangled and metal clanged. They'd opened the lady's cell door. "I brought clean clothes, but you'll need to wash up first. Sidney, do you have a tub? And where can she change?"

"Wilfred, get the privacy screen." Footsteps, a door opened and shut. "Sorry, Hazel. She'll have to change there in the cell, but we'll preserve your daughter's modesty."

"Hmph. I come to Silver for the masquerade ball, and end up tending my trigger-happy daughter in jail. With a strange man."

Kade wanted to say something but he couldn't make his mouth move yet. The lady could learn a thing or two about target identification.

"Mama, they were trying to rob the bank!"

"Well, let them. They could've shot you full of holes and I'd be coming for your funeral. Do you know how many gray hairs you've given me this morning? And where are your spectacles, young lady?"

"I lost them during the robbery."

Keys jangled, a metal clang and a squeak—had to be the jail cell door opening. "Brung the privacy screen."

"Put it right here," Mrs. Gardner said. "Your man is unconscious so he won't be able to see you, and we'll shield you from the other two men."

"Not much room back here," Iris grumbled. "Mama, you'll have to leave so I have room to change. I can unlace everything myself."

How could the Big Gun in the Sky do this to him? A woman was going to get naked right next to him and he could barely move a muscle. Talk about hell on earth. Clothing rustled and he heard her moving around, probably bumping against the privacy screen. He had to look. He just *had* to look.

Slowly, he tilted his head slightly to the right and willed his eyes to open. What a sight to behold. She was bent over with the top of her head not two feet from him, and he had the sweetest view of her ample cleavage near to bursting out of that corset. He groaned, whether from the hot dagger that seemed stuck through his eyeballs, or the glorious sight to behold, he didn't know.

She glanced up, wide-eyed, then straightened and clutched her dress against her breasts. "Mama! He's awake, and I'm... I'm unpresentable!"

"Oh my stars!" Mrs. Gardner spluttered. "Sidney, we simply must get her to the boardinghouse to change."

Kade closed his eyes again, willing his head to stop pounding so much. At least it was a beautiful woman who shot him in the head—many men had tried and failed. He wished he could've touched the blond curl at the nape of her neck that had escaped from the tightly coiled bun. Her bosom, ah, he'd remember forever, so rounded and soft. That one glance etched itself firmly in his mind.

More skirts rustling. More clanging, and people moving around all over the place, in and out of the cell.

"All right," Mrs. Gardner said. "You're done up now, but you look a bit pale."

"Mama, what a mess I'm in."

"No talking about the case, Miss Gardner," admonished the sheriff.

"Are you marrying this one?" the sheriff asked. He chuckled, but Kade didn't think it was so funny. Seemed like a pretty strange question.

"Sidney!" Miss Gardner yelped, hurting Kade's head. "Is

Vivvie at the boardinghouse? She'll want to know, especially if I have to stay here."

Vivvie? That was his sister's name. How many Vivvies could there be in Owyhee County? Kade hadn't seen her for four years. He managed to open his eyes, but stars danced in the daylight. He blinked softly, but even that caused the throbbing in his head to worsen so he shut them. The cot was as bad as sleeping on a box of rocks. Time to take inventory. He flexed his biceps one at a time, then his leg muscles. No pain there, probably no broken bones.

She must have shot him in the head but it couldn't be too bad or he'd be dead, and there sure weren't any angels in the vicinity. Or demons, as would most likely be the case. But if his sister was in town, he wanted to see her.

"Look, Mama! He's moving."

"Do you know who he is?" Mrs. Gardner asked.

"I'm afraid not. I didn't have my spectacles on so he was all blurry, but I knew by his posture and movement that he's not a bank customer."

Kade licked his parched lips. "I'm awake," he croaked as he touched his bandaged head. "Someone want to tell me about this?"

A man's bootsteps neared. "Mister, the doc says for you not to move too much and don't talk, either, until you're good and ready. We have plenty of time."

Kade opened his eyes, but focusing was too much work and he closed them again.

"No, we don't," said Miss Gardner. "I still have to balance the day's ledgers."

The man had called her Iris Gardner. Kade thought about that. And Vivvie, his sister. "Iris Gardner. Cute little girl."

"He's talking! You know me?"

"Ornery as a magpie."

A man chuckled. "He knows her." *The sheriff speaking.*

"That's our Iris," her mother said, "especially when

143

Vivvie's around."

Kade really wanted to know if this Vivvie was his sister. Gunmen weren't supposed to miss their families, but then none of them had his family. They had always been close.

"Who *are* you?" Miss Gardner asked him.

A Note from the Author

If you'd like to continue the fun ride, go to the **Much Ado About Miners** website for all purchase links. I love to hear from readers, and I'd be grateful if you'd post a review at the major sites.

About the Author

Jacquie Rogers grew up on a dairy farm outside of Homedale, Idaho, in Owyhee County. She has fond memories of riding horseback all over the hills where her western historical romance series, _Hearts of Owyhee,_ is set. Those hills held exciting adventures both real and imagined. She currently lives in suburbia with her IT Guy (also has a license to sleep with him), daughter, and four grandsons. Their home is ruled by The Cat Annie, a feral rescue, who enjoys tromping on the keyboard in the midst of action or love scenes.

Besides the Hearts of Owyhee series, Jacquie also writes a traditional western series, _Muleskinners_. Under the house name of Ford Fargo, she writes collaborative westerns with Western Fictioneers. She also writes fantasy romance and whatever else tickles her fancy.

Jacquie is a member of Romance Writers of America and Western Fictioneers. Her books have garnered several awards, the most recent being the LASR Book of the Month for **Mail-Order Tangle**, a duet with Caroline Clemmons. **Much Ado About Mavericks** has been featured at Claudia's Book Talk.

You're welcome to subscribe to her newsletter, the Pickle Barrel Gazette, and join her Facebook group, Jacquie Rogers' Pickle Barrel Bar & Books.

Contact

Website | www.jacquiergers.com
Twitter |@jacqierogers
Facebook | www.facebook.com/jacquierogersauthor
Pinterest | www.pinterest.com/jacquierogers
Google+:https://plus.google.com/+JacquieRogers/posts

Other books by Jacquie Rogers

Hearts of Owyhee series
Much Ado About Madams
Much Ado About Marshals
Much Ado About Miners
Much Ado About Mavericks
Coming soon:
Much Ado About Mustangs

With Caroline Clemmons
Mail-Order Tangle

See Jacquie's other titles on her website:
www.jacquierogers.com.

LITTLE BEAR AND THE LADIES

The Fairy Saga

by

NATIONAL BESTSELLING AUTHOR

Dani Haviland

With so many females, what's a bachelor to do?

Copyright © 2015 by Dani Haviland

Book Description

North Carolina, late autumn, 1782. Little Bear, a Scottish emigrant trapper, has just made a deal with a Hessian colonel: he's purchased the survivors of their raid on a small Indian village. The bachelor isn't sure what he's to do with them, but knows he must keep them hidden from the greedy mercenary sergeant who is looking for his stash of gold...and the good-looking women who he's now responsible for.

Praise

"If you love to lose yourself in large fantasy novels, you're going to love this series."

"I absolutely LOVE Dani Haviland's work. This author has the ability to pull you into the story with excellent use of dialect, wonderful descriptions, and other techniques that bring her stories to life."

Chapter 9 (partial)
The Good Book

Backwoods of North Carolina
Late autumn, 1782

They settled down comfortably after dinner, tired but everyone with a full belly. The low glow and warmth of the campfire was an extra source of comfort to them: they could sleep tonight without fear.

Morning Star took over setting up the bedroom accommodations from She Bear. "I'm going to sleep with Little Bear tonight," she told her stepdaughter softly. "Will you keep the babies safe and bring me Shooting Star if he's hungry?"

She Bear nodded and smiled. "Is he going to be my father now?" she asked hopefully. She really liked the gentle man. He could never replace her first father but, just as Morning Star was her new mother, she could love him as a parent, too.

"I hope so," Morning Star answered truthfully.

She knew he liked her—their close sleeping proximity the past two nights had made it evident. She didn't wake him from his squirming, thrusting dreams. She enjoyed them, too. She wanted to turn to him at those times, the times when he was asleep and not guarded, but that wouldn't have been fair to him. He didn't know what he was doing, although a couple of times he had awaken right at the end. She pretended to be asleep every time. Yes, he was a good provider, and would make a good husband, father, and lover.

Little Bear stayed away from the group while the beds were being set up. This time, Morning Star was arranging the blankets and putting his off to the side. Yes, they had a fire tonight so they wouldn't have to snuggle together. He sighed at his loss. He really wanted to be with her, but didn't know how to ask her.

She had lost her husband not even a week before. He didn't know the appropriate grieving period and didn't want to insult her by asking her too soon. And he was a bit timid, too. Maybe next winter would be long enough. Hopefully, he'd be brave enough to ask her by then.

Morning Star sat with her back to the fire, nursing Shooting Star. Little Bear walked up to the fire and stood on the other side of it from her. The others were already covered with blankets, although not necessarily asleep. He heard Rachel telling her son Full Moon to quit biting her; he was teething. She Bear was singing a song to Baby Brother, his squawking getting quieter as her song slowed down. "Ring around the rosies, pocket full of posies, ashes, ashes…"

Morning Star stood up and walked over to She Bear, bent over, and handed Shooting Star to her. "Bring him to me if he wakes up and is hungry, all right?" she asked softly, her words too low from Little Bear to hear.

She Bear nodded, took her youngest brother in her arms, and snuggled him between her, Baby Brother, and Later. It felt so good to have a warm fire, a full belly, and a man to watch over them. Life was good again. And now her first mother had her father up in heaven with her.

Morning Star slowly walked away from her children to Little Bear's bed. He was still standing by the fire, poking the embers to make sure the fire burned low through the night and didn't flare up and burn itself out. He watched her as she lifted his blanket aside, pulled off her dress, climbed in, and covered herself up. Gulp. She was ready. He wouldn't have to wait a year.

He walked to the bed, turning one last time to see if he was being watched by the others. Rachel was snoring softly and She Bear was stifling a giggle. She knew what was going on and was evidently fine with it or she'd be crying. He bent over, took off his moccasins, and pulled his shirt off over his head. He knelt next to the bedding and performed his last act as a single man:

untied the knot of his breechclout belt.

Even though he had just been out in the cold, his body was hot; only his chest was chilly. Morning Star snuggled close and rubbed her hands all over his shoulders, down the outside of his arms, feeling his strength, smelling his musk. She dipped her head and rubbed her face into his collar bone, hoping that he'd start touching her. She was aching all over. And it wasn't from the long ride. She wanted him to caress her like her husband had. She missed Number Two, but knew that he was gone. He had taken her as his wife just days after his first wife had died; she was sure that he'd want her to do the same. He had said once that the hole in his heart had been filled quickly and fully by her. Hopefully, Little Bear could do the same for her.

Little Bear was having a hard time keeping his hands from her. He enjoyed her gentle strokes, the soft, warm hands on his upper body. He wasn't sure what he should do next. He knew 'what' to do; he was trained as a doctor and even had a woman once when he and his classmates had gone to the whorehouse. He was drunk at the time and didn't remember too much. He did remember the row afterwards and the loss of his best friend, knifed by a jealous customer. The woman was a whore and anyone could buy her, but the old lawyer thought that she was his and made sure Jedediah never came back to her, stabbing him in the stomach until he bled out. He shook his head; not the right kind of thought to be having at a time like this.

Morning Star saw Little Bear shake his head. Maybe she was wrong; maybe he didn't want to be with her. "Don't you want me?" she asked sadly, embarrassed at her brazenness.

"Uh, yes, very much yes," he answered, and put his hand on her hip. He suddenly realized that she must have thought that when he was shaking his head to clear it of the bad thoughts, that he was telling her no. "That is, if you'll have me," he added. "I don't have much to offer, not even a home, but I'll not let you starve, and I'll do my best to keep you warm and safe."

"What more could any woman ask," she said, holding back

151

the words, 'except to be loved.'

"And I'll love you, too," he added, then brought his hand to the side of her face and touched her gently. He leaned close to her, smelled her neck, and then buried his whole face in the nook between her jaw and collarbone—a place that seemed made just for a man's snuggles and kisses. He wasn't used to kissing. Shoot, he'd never kissed a woman and practicing on the back of his hand as a teenager didn't count. He rubbed his nose against the soft skin of her neck and realized that the kissing was coming naturally. His lips were touching her, moving by themselves toward her mouth.

Morning Star was having a hard time containing herself. She remembered how slow and gentle Number Two had been on their first night. She was eager then, too. But this was different. She could tell Little Bear hadn't been with a woman lately, if ever at all. He was a good man and probably wouldn't mind if she guided him. After all, if they were to be married—and by the feel of his swollen manhood, that would definitely happen tonight—then they would have many more nights together where he could lead the way to pleasure.

She turned her head so her mouth was on his. His lips were tense; he was scared. She left her mouth closed and relaxed her lips, letting his follow suit. Her hand drifted down the outside of his arms to his hip, gently sweeping around his back to grasp his buttocks. He instinctively pushed himself closer, his mouth hearing the call of urgency that his loins were screaming. She reached back around and guided his hand to her breast. Her son had drained her, but she knew that she was never totally empty. She wanted him there, too. She arched her back at the same time as she pushed his head toward her chest.

"Please," she whispered, not wanting to beg, but knowing that she'd have to guide him for their first night, their wedding night, together.

Little Bear felt her hand urging him to her breast. Did she want to suckle him? Was that what husbands and wives did? He shook his head, then bent sideways to take her nipple in his mouth. To hell with what he had read or what he thought. She knew what to do, and if he shut down his brain and listened to his body, he was sure to do the right thing.

Oh, no! Morning Star feared. No, wait… momentary panic averted. He shook his head when she urged him to suckle her: he didn't want to. No, it must have been something else because he immediately followed her directions. "Oh, my," escaped her lips as he found his target.

"Hmm?" Little Bear questioned with his mouth full of nipple. Now that he had it in his mouth, he didn't want to let it go, at least not yet. The milk that was coming from her breast was so sweet and the feel of them joining, at least there, was a good start at letting go of his inhibitions.

"I'm fine, but…" Morning Star lost her words as he let go of her nipple and crossed to her other breast and resumed his suckling. "Oh, my," she repeated then giggled.

"Am I doing it right?" he asked, embarrassed at his insecurity.

"Uh, huh, but, when you're ready, I mean, when you want, you can climb on top of me. We can do it more than once."

Little Bear rubbed his hips against hers, pressing his firmness against her, letting her know wordlessly that he was ready. He rolled on top of her, then remembered his gaffe with the prostitute. *"Use yer elbows, dolt!" she had screeched. "Yer crushin' the wind outta me!"*

He put his hands on the ground and lifted up away from her. There was enough glow from the firelight that he could see her body under his. "You're beautiful," he said, and bent his face to hers, giving her a full-mouthed kiss that seemed so right to share. Morning Star wiggled her bottom under his, urging him to continue with the penetration.

"Now?" he asked, hoping that she'd say yes.

"Yes, yes, now, now," she squeaked, then reached in between their bellies, grabbed his cock, and placed it between

153

her legs. "Whoa!" she exclaimed. "You're huge!"

"Is that bad?" he asked, and started to pull away—or at least thought that maybe he should. Now that he was almost inside her, he wanted to continue. He was using intense concentration skills to keep from thrusting all the way into her: his mating instincts were definitely active.

"No, no, go ahead," she said, pulling his hips towards her. "You'll fit just fine."

~*~

Morning Star was radiant the next morning, her wedding night glow only exceeded by the grin that Little Bear wore. He tried to suppress it every time he realized it was there, but there was nothing he could do. Well, not nothing; he could probably think about something sad, but he didn't want to do that, not today, not ever!

Rachel shuffled her feet as she neared the fire, wearing a morose frown and emanating a bad attitude that Little Bear found hard to ignore. Morning Star wasn't blind to the dour mood either. The newlywed couple's eyes met; they knew what it was.

Jealousy.

Now what were they going to do? The chance for Rachel to find a mate in the next six months was nil. They had to stay hidden for everyone's safety. The gold-hunting sergeant was bound to be on the lookout for them. And the more they traveled—a small Indian tribe with lots of babies—the easier they would be to spot. Besides, the first flakes of winter would be flying in weeks if not days, and they would be hindered by the snow. They had to remain where they were and construct permanent housing as quickly as possible.

It was a disaster waiting to happen, jealousy infused with sexual frustration. She'd have to figure something out or Rachel would make everyone miserable.

154

As they worked on stage one of their home building—picking up and stacking the wood that littered the site—Morning Star asked, "Little Bear, do you believe in God?"

"Yes, of course I do. I mean, I know Him as God, but I also believe He's who the Indians call the Great Father or the Great Spirit. Why do you ask?"

Instead of answering, she asked another question. "Have you ever read the Bible?"

"Yes, I've read The Good Book several times, however I don't have a copy of it now. Do you have a question? I mean, do you think that we have to have a Bible or a priest or preacher to have a valid marriage?" Little Bear wanted to remind her that she didn't have either one of them when she married Number Two, but surely she knew that, and it wasn't a problem.

"Did you ever notice how many men in the Bible had more than one wife? I mean, most of them did. One of the reasons was because so many had been killed in battle. There weren't enough men for all of the women."

"Yes, I believe you're right," he answered cautiously. Then he realized what she was suggesting. He sighed deeply. "You think I should have two wives?"

Morning Star nodded her head. "If they do it in The Good Book, then it's fine with me, too. As long as it's agreeable with you and her, I think it'd be best for everyone. I know she likes you. Not as much as I like you, maybe, but good enough." Morning Star started to giggle. "And she's not as noisy as I am when making love. You might like that part."

"No," he answered, then saw the scared look on her face. "No, I like your noises. Do you want to ask her or shall I? I mean, you might want to suggest it to her first. If she thinks it will work, I'll ask her."

"Great!" Morning Star said, then popped over to Rachel, pulling her aside to discuss the issue away from She Bear.

"Now what have you got yourself into, man." Little Bear looked up to the sky. "Very funny, Lord. I wanted a wife, so You gave me two. I wanted a child, so you gave me five."

"At least five," Rachel said, as she walked up beside him. "Do you want me tonight or do you want a few more nights alone with Morning Star first?"

(Find out what happens next in *Little Bear and the Ladies, available now on Amazon.*)

A Note from the Author

If you enjoyed this excerpt from *Little Bear and the Ladies*, you can meet Little Bear for the first time in *Naked in the Winter Wind.* There's also more about him, Rachel, Morning Star and others in *Dances Naked*, third book in The Fairies Saga.

Please (pretty please) recommend and review the books.

You can contact the author at dani.haviland@gmail.com with your comments.

About the Author

Dani Haviland began writing late in life, but old age hasn't slowed her down. An avid researcher and photographer, she traveled to Sydney, Australia in 2014 to study the land, climate, and to experience sailing on a tall ship (massive seasickness-ugh) for the next big novel in her series, *Fairies Down Under*, the tale of a time traveler who winds up on the First Fleet of convicts, bound for the newly discovered and barely explored Botany Bay, Australia.

From Connecticut to Arizona (early years) to Alaska (past 23 years) to her current residence in Oregon, Dani never fades in her search for beauty and awe. Check out some of her photos: www.danihaviland.com and Pinterest.

And watch for novellas to be released in between her major (over 150,000 words) novels.

Contact

Author site: danihaviland.com

Amazon author page: http://www.amazon.com/Dani-Haviland/e/B0054R44KQ

On Twitter: @dani_haviland

Facebook: facebook.com/dani.haviland

Blog: danihaviland.blogspot.com

Tumblr: DaniLovesPretties

Other books by Dani Haviland

Naked in the Winter Wind: Who, and when was she? And was this mountain man really her husband? Fountain of Youth water and a big case of amnesia confound life. Book One.

Ha'Penny Jenny A novella about a sweet (and psychic) young lass of 1780s North Carolina, her trials, fears, and discoveries. Light-hearted, sweet story, suitable for all ages. Book One and a half.

Aye, I am a Fairy: Where was mom? Could that young woman who showed up in the emergency room then disappeared really be her? And who was this hunky British Lord who said he was there to help her? Leah meets James and questions and sparks fly. Book Two.

Dances Naked: Lost in the backwoods of 18th century North Carolina, Marty, an amiable British Lord is rescued by three Indians. How would he find his way back to The Trees, the portal through time? Book Three.

The Great Big Fairy: Benji was born in the 18th century, but came to the 20th century as a youth. Now all grown up, he wants to return to his natal time. Will he make? And once there, will he be able to remain? Falling in love had its complications. Book Four.

COCKTAIL COVE

Frankly, My Dear Series

by

USA TODAY BEST SELLING AUTHOR

Jennifer Saints

A Southern Steam Novel

Copyright © 2013 Jenni Leigh Grizzle

Book Description

When life shakes you up and pours you over the rocks…

Socialite Nikita Derringer is hiding from the mob because of a deal her ex made with the devil, that she accidentally did her ex in with her designer heels, is… beside the point.

Guilt ridden developer Ben Harding walked away from his lucrative big city job and is searching for redemption in the quiet solitude of his grandfather's sacred fishing cove. But fate has something else in mind for them at Cocktail Cove. Throw in sex therapy for the masses, a bear of a dog, the deep end of passion and you've got a potent mix guaranteed to ignite your senses and fill your heart with love and laughter.

Praise

"I just love everything about this series, I can't wait for more. It is well written with great characters."

~Heidi Gillespie

"It was a roller coaster ride. I fell in love with the characters."

~Kim
Hammerling

Excerpt from Cocktail Cove by Jennifer Saints…

Ben hit the nail with such force that it rammed flush with the board with one drive. Since his buttering up Friday night he'd been brewing a potent stew. How could Gram have sold the land? He slammed two more nails home. It was a good thing the Cocktail Cove crew had partied themselves out and left. Otherwise, Ben was in just the mood to swim out there and knock a hole in the bottom of their boats. Hell and damnation, from the way the estrogen troops sounded you'd have thought he'd been a Mussolini running their lives.

Bear had been suspiciously absent since leaving him and James at the campfire last night and Ben wondered if he should go looking for the mutt. As if on cue, Ben heard Bear barking and running up to the cabin.

"Well, it's about time you showed up," Ben shouted, working on another nail.

"Help."

At the soft, shaky voice, Ben jerked his head up and lost his balance. He fell sideways, barely catching himself before landing flat on his face on the cabin's sub floor. As it was, he ended up eye level with the woman's chest. The woman was tall, and a mess. Dark mud caked her hair, face, and shirt which must have once been a soft blue. She wavered as if she was too drunk to stay upright and the rest of her wasn't in any better shape.

"What in the hell happened to you?" Ben sat up.

"I don't know," she said, putting a dirty hand to the side of her head. Her blue eyes were the only part of her he could discern for sure. He'd heard of cornflower blue eyes before, but he'd never seen them—not until now. They shimmered with tears, and looked at him in utter confusion. Well, hell this was the last thing he needed. She looked like a Cocktail Cove reject. Something must have gone wrong between the champagne and

161

the funky foreplay.

Ben set down his hammer. Already short on patience, he exhaled in exasperation. "Okay, lady. Let's walk this horse a different way. Who are you?"

She looked to the side, winced and groaned as she did. "What? What horse?"

Ben rolled a kink of tension in his neck. "Just tell me who you are."

She looked at him and swayed on her feet. "I don't know."

"You don't remember?" Was she that drunk? Ben muttered to himself as he jumped down to catch the woman before she toppled into the dirt. Scooping her up, he looked around the clearing to see if anyone else was with her. As her head rolled against his arm, he saw a long gash slashing from her temple almost to the back of her neck, and what he thought was mud, was actually dirt and dried blood.

"My God, woman. What happened to you?" Hurrying now, Ben rushed over to the old hut he was living in and laid her on the couch. Snatching a towel, he ran some cool water from the faucet and began washing the woman's face. Her eyes fluttered open, then filled with tears.

"Hurt," she whispered. "Head hurts. Need help."

"Okay," Ben said, laying his hand on her cheek. "I'll get you help. Maybe you'll remember what happened by the time we get to the hospital. Just hang in there and relax." It was a relief to realize he needed to take her to the hospital. He grabbed his keys, his wallet, and a pillow for the woman, and carried her out to the car.

Six hours later, he was sure his sanity was slipping with every second that ticked. People were packed into the ER waiting room like hens in a chicken house, and the staff ran around like chickens with their heads cut off. The woman he'd brought in still wasn't done with the tests the doctors had ordered and she still didn't know who she was.

As soon as the woman was placed into a hospital room, he

162

could entertain the idea of going home. Until then, he was stuck. For the past two hours, "Ten Hot Bedroom Tricks Guaranteed to Satisfy," had glared at him from the cover of a magazine. The teen reading it sat directly across from him and didn't look old enough to have a learner's permit for anything. She reminded him of his sisters when growing up and he had to trap his hands under his arms to keep himself from snatching the magazine away and replacing it with a *Harry Potter* book. These days, kids got in over their heads long before they were ready to have their ears wet.

He turned his attention to the bouncing infant on his right who was being kept happy with Cheerios from his mother. Ben had never seen such a half-eaten gummed up mess in his life. The baby and the chair arms between them were covered in gook. But the little tyke had a way of begging for more Cheerios with his innocent blues that not even Scrooge could have resisted.

He winked at the boy and the boy gurgled back, jumping so hard that he flew from his mother's hold.

Ben caught the boy before he toppled to the floor. "Whoa there, cowboy."

The baby gurgled and offered Ben a gummed Cheerio.

"Oh my gosh! Thank you," the mother gasped. "He's getting harder and harder to hold on to. Now look what he's done. You've mashed Cheerios all over your arm." She wrestled with a diaper bag, pulled out a baby wipe, and held it up. "I'm so sorry."

Ben handed the baby back, surprised to find that he wasn't necessarily in a hurry to do so. "No problem," he said to the harried mother, taking the baby wipe. He realized that he hadn't seen her though he'd been sitting next to her for two hours. She appeared worn out, and worry clouded her eyes. Ben smiled at her. "It has to be hard keeping him happy in this coop. You're doing a great job."

"Most people would be complaining about the Cheerios.

Thanks. Chance is easy because he isn't mobile yet. It's the other two, Scott and Allie that are hard to handle. At three and four, they've decided they're Jackie Chan. They both have a fever. My husband's seeing the doctor with them."

Ben remembered his worry when his sisters got sick. "I hope it's nothing more than an ear ache or a weak virus."

"Me, too. You just don't know how fragile and precious kids are until they're your own. You have kids?"

"Not yet," Ben said. He then blinked when he realized the glimmer of regret he felt behind those words. The squeak of shoes on the linoleum grabbed his attention and Ben looked up, hoping he'd soon be able to see the woman he'd brought in, even though he didn't have a clue as to what he would say.

"Uh, Mister…" The hospital worker moved her three-inch, blue nails down the page of the chart she held and frowned. "Mr. Doe?"

Ben released his breath, disappointed. No one responded and the worker called again. Still no response. Finally, the clerk slapped the chart against her hip and said, "Is anybody here with Jane Doe?"

Jane Doe? Is that what they had named the woman he'd brought in?

Ben stood. "Are you talking about the tall blonde who has been here for hours?"

"Don't know nothin' about tall and blonde, but the time matches. Come with me Mr. Doe."

"Harding," Ben said, following the woman. But he didn't hold any hope that she'd get his name right. It had taken thirty minutes to convince the ER admissions clerk that he didn't know the name of the woman whom he'd brought in. It would probably take twice that long to convince this one that he *did* know his own name.

"As in Harding Doe, or as in Doe Harding?

"Neither. The name's Ben Harding." He followed the woman to a little cubicle and she sat down behind a computer.

164

Her nails were as long as the keyboard and had Yin and Yang symbols painted on the tops of each one.

"I need to fill in the missing blanks to admit Mrs. Doe to the hospital and get her insurance information. Who is her carrier?"

"I don't know?"

"Address?"

"Don't know"

"Phone?"

"Don't know."

"What *can* you tell me about her?"

"She has blue eyes. She's about five-nine; she has a gash on the left side of her head, and she doesn't know who she is."

The clerk leaned back in her chair and tapped a long nail on the top of her computer. She didn't look happy. Ben supposed his answers put her Yin and Yang out of balance.

"It says here that she fell from your boat and hit her head."

Ben groaned. "Nope, I said that she might have fallen from *a* boat. It all depends. She was muddy, but not soaking wet. I don't own a boat, at least nothing but a canoe. And I don't know how she was hurt. It was a guess. She found me. There were these boats in the cove scaring my fish and—"

The woman held up her hand. "I don't have time for long stories. I got a room full of people to put in this computer. As soon as we get this done, I can send you up to Jane's room. Ben gave her his information and handed her his insurance card, already enjoying the snafus that would cause in the hospital's bookkeeping department.

"She's on the third floor. Check in with the nurse's station."

"Thanks." Ben stood and quickly escaped the jaws of ER lunacy. But as he approached the elevator, his steps began to drag. What did you say to someone who didn't know who they were, and didn't know who you were, either? He should just go home now. He turned to leave.

A pink lady from the gift shop with hair teased into a silver halo wrinkled her painted-on eyebrows, and peered at him through Mr. Magoo bifocals. "You look like a young man who needs to take a gift to somebody special."

"I do?" Ben stopped in his tracks.

"Yes. The gift shop is right this way."

"Thanks" he said, taking the volunteer's lead. Flowers were always good. He'd take the woman some flowers and leave. Now that he had a plan, it didn't take him long. The minute he stepped through the door, he knew what he wanted. He passed by all the showy vases of roses and reached for a teapot as cornflower blue as the woman's eyes. In it, a miniature garden of blue and white flowers had been planted. He made his way to the cashier, but it seemed his shopping wasn't over. A *Harry Potter* book screamed at him, and the looks of a soft plastic baby's book about red fire engines rang Ben's bell. He snatched them up, paid for it all and made a quick trip back to the ER waiting room to deliver his presents before going up to the woman's room.

~*~

Doesn't know her name.

Doesn't know what happened.

Mild temporal lobe swelling.

Blunt trauma. No hematoma.

Hairline fracture. Very rare. Very lucky.

Comments from the hospital staff swirled in Nik's head. She'd been a one-woman *Ripley's Believe It Or Not* on a stretcher for hours with everyone whispering behind her back. Apparently amnesia was an oddity at which even the hospital janitor and administrator had to peek. She'd been poked and prodded from head to toe. Her head throbbed, her eyes burned, her body ached, but the worst part of it all was the lying. She couldn't relax, partly because she feared her lie being discovered. But mostly because an unreasonable fear clawed at her.

The one thing she could tell the truth about was her sense of

166

panic and her fear, which worked in her favor because it made them wonder if she'd been attacked and dumped in the woods. And that in itself was partly true, wasn't it? Had Tom planned to dump her somewhere, or had she imagined it?

Everything from Tom blocking the road until she'd awaken this morning in the woods with a huge black dog cuddled up against her was a jumbled mess of images and feelings. She wanted to shut her eyes and pretend everything was fine, but she couldn't.

Had there been a man with a gun? Tom had said a hitman was after them. Had she imagined he'd found Tom and her? If he had, why was she alive then? To her way of thinking, if there had been a hitman, he couldn't find her if no one knew her name. She wasn't exactly lying about her amnesia, only just the part about knowing who she was.

Flashes of things came to her. Her argument with Tom. The dog. Her heels hitting Tom's head as she flew over the seat. Had there been a man with a gun? Squeezing her eyes shut, she saw herself as she ran from Tom's body. She hadn't seen blood or a bullet, but she remembered terror and pain.

All night long she heard Tom's voice over and over again in her mind. *I can get my hands on the land now. I tell you she's not an issue anymore and won't be ever again.* Those words, plus his surprise when she'd touched him on the shoulder, told her volumes the longer she thought about it. The doctors said she had three wounds on her head...as if she'd been hit several times. Something like that didn't like happen in a single fall. But she didn't dare ask specific questions, because they'd then wonder if she could remember.

If there was a hitman, wouldn't going to the police make it easier for him to find her? It was all so confusing and her head hurt so much.

She couldn't even go to her friends. That would put them in danger. She could go to her brother, Nicholas, in South America. Disappear by helping dig up relics in the jungle? Camp out and

167

die from malaria or those weird flies that lay eggs in your skin or a vampire bat that—Nik shuddered.

She'd rather check into the Ritz-Carlton and take her chances.

But that would have to wait until she was well. So, for now, she'd pretend total amnesia and delay dealing with the awful realities of her situation until later. Liz and Ezzy already thought she was taking a trip back to London with her nephews, and her nephews didn't know she'd been coming after them. So nobody would really "miss" her for a couple of weeks, which was a really scary realization when she considered what Tom had planned to do to her.

The door to her room opened and she cried out.

"God, I'm sorry. Uh, I'll, uh, go—"

Nik clutched her throat and swallowed the fear clogging it as she realized the man who'd brought her to the hospital stood in the doorway. She recognized his voice, if not him. He'd been very blurry this morning. He wasn't now. "No. It's okay. I, uh, you just surprised me. I didn't know you were still here."

"I couldn't leave without knowing if you were going to be all right or not." The man shrugged, still standing at the threshold.

She cleared her throat. "Um, come in unless you're here to give me another test. I don't think I can take another one today."

"No tests. Bear ate the pop quiz anyway." He sauntered into the room, and the full effect of him smacked her in the face. Worn jeans and a faded green shirt hugged his every muscle. His sun-kissed hair and sexy scruff framed his strong, vibrant features. But what hit the hardest were his eyes. They were a deep blue, full of concern and... made her feel...safe? But *how*? She didn't know him, his name, or anything about him—except that he was completely un-Tom-like.

"Bear?" Nik asked, wondering how she'd found the brain-width to reply. Some men defied words. He defied...rational thought. *Get a grip, Nik.* The blow to her head had obviously skewed her X and Y axis and left her unbalanced.

"My dog. That beast you followed to the cabin this morning."

She nodded.

"Are you all right?" The man leaned closer.

"Just peachy," she said as a wave of heat flushed from her below her navel to her scalp. She wanted to pull the covers over her head and die. What perverse twist of fate had arranged for this prime specimen of modern man to meet her when she lay splattered at rock bottom? And why did her heretofore latent libido suddenly revive itself? In the months since her separation and even counting a year or two before her radar screen labeled "real desire" had remained blipless. Now it was out-beeping her heart monitor.

"Peachy?" He lifted a brow. "Rough day?"

"One I'd rather forget," she said and then winced. An amnesiac wouldn't be wishing to forget. "That is, uh, if I could remember things I'm sure I'd want to forget it. This morning is kind of a blur. Did you tell me your name?"

He smiled. It was mega-watt. "You know, I don't remember."

She inanely nodded again.

"My name's Ben." He set a teapot on her bedside table. "This is for you."

A teapot? He brought her a teapot planter? Not roses, but a teapot with delicate blue and white flowers in it. Having received extravagant gifts all of her life, Nik was completely captured by the teapot.

"Thank you." She spoke softly, running her fingers over the ceramic. It was smooth and still warm from his hands, comforting and…special. Two things she hadn't experienced in forever. "They're beautiful," she whispered. Her eyes burned.

169

A Note from the Author

Thank you so much for reading Cocktail Cove. If you enjoyed this chapter, please read the entire book and leave an honest review.

About the Author

USA Today Bestselling author, Jennifer St. Giles, aka Jennifer Saints, J.L. Saint is no ordinary Georgia Peach. She's a Golden Heart, three-time Maggie, two-time National Reader's Choice, Marlene, RT Reviewer's Choice and Daphne du Maurier award-winning author. Jenni writes in multiple genres, including: romance, paranormal, contemporary, historical and military and time travel. She is a passionate patriot, event planner and the Vice-President of a charitable foundation which helps women and children's causes. Jenni believes fervently in following your dreams and never giving up.

Contact

Jenniferstgiles.com http://jenniferstgiles.com/content/

Twitter @jenniferstgiles or @jennifer_saints

Facebook https://www.facebook.com/jenniferstgiles

Other books by Jennifer Saints

Wild Irish Ride
Smooth Irish Seduction
Hard Irish Luck
A Weldon Family Christmas
Hot Irish Lass
Weldon Brothers Bundle

Other books by Jennifer St. Giles

Touch a Dark Wolf

Lure of the Wolf

Kiss of Darkness

Bride of the Wolf

The Mistress of Trevelyan

His Dark Desires

Midnight Secrets

Darkest Dreams

Silken Shadows

Books by JL Saint

Collateral Damage

Tactical Deception

STIRRING IT UP

by

USA TODAY BEST SELLING AUTHOR

Love With a Twist~Valentine Romance Collection

Mary Leo

Copyright © 2013 Mary Leo

Book Description

When a gypsy's prediction begins to come true, Rose Cupido dismisses it as a coincidence, but when a past estranged boyfriend shows up reminding her of the love she once felt for him, Rose can't help wondering if that gypsy had true magical powers.

Praise

"I really enjoyed the raw emotion of this author... brilliant!"
~Henry Nardi

"Stirring It Up was an amazing read! Mary Leo wrote another great book...."
~ Chocolate Thunder

Chapter One

It wasn't as if Rose-Marie Cupido had actually believed she would find her one true love during this past year, she'd simply been hopeful that it could possibly happen. Everything else the gypsy had predicted had come true, including the wild success of *With a Twist,* the martini bar and bistro she and her two best girlfriends had opened. The fact that she was now listed as one of San Diego's top ten chefs, and the unexpected letter she'd received from her estranged father wanting to mend their relationship had all been predictions the gypsy had made, but finding her true love before February fourteenth?

Impossible!

Besides, Rose truly didn't see how she could fit a romance into her already busy schedule, no matter how badly she may want or need one. What with all her responsibilities of running the kitchen, ordering the food, and cooking six nights a week, squeezing in a budding romance seemed highly unlikely.

She had all but given up on the love prediction, convinced it would never happen, until Maximilian Rosso walked into the bar looking for his cousin, Jasmine.

She knew him instantly, knew the curve of his chin, the shape of his lips, the deep amber of his eyes, but most of all she knew the swagger of his walk. No other boy or man she'd ever known walked with that much cool. He'd had that strut since they were kids and she was glad to see it hadn't changed.

All at once, the proximity of his tantalizing body caused the gypsy's red crystal heart sitting on the bar to glow like crazy, and all at once Rose felt completely dumbstruck, not knowing what to do or say. The likelihood that Max could fall in love with her in less than thirteen days seemed about as probable as her not stressing over every meal that came out of her kitchen.

The crystal had already cast its glow on some hot cutie that Jasmine was all happy about, but if Max was truly the one for Rose, she had her work cut out for her. For one thing, he barely knew she existed.

Just last year, Rose and her two best friends, Jasmine and Daisy had decided to get all glammed up on Valentine's Day to make it a fun night instead of moping around because they didn't have dates. They decided on dinner and drinks at Harbor House in San Diego's Seaport Village, then a walk along the boardwalk to their next stop when they came across the gypsy with her folding table, shiny baubles and colorful silk scarves. Rose caught the amazing red glow of the large crystal heart perched on her table and went directly for it as if she had no choice in the matter. When she reached for it, she realized that Jasmine and Daisy were doing the exact same thing.

Rose hadn't thought her friends had even noticed the gypsy, and certainly not the dazzling crystal that seemed to have a life of its own. A red so deep and so vibrant she felt sure it was magical.

"Never seen it choose three before," the gypsy woman remarked, almost giggling as she spoke. Her gray eyes sparkled with excitement, as her face took on a radiant warm glow. Rose was at once apprehensive of this assertive woman who appeared as though she were dressed for a costume party rather than someone to be taken as a serious medium.

Still, Rose and her friends lingered in front of her small table, each mesmerized by the glistening crystal, and the excitement that seemed to be percolating within the beguiling woman.

Looking back, Rose thought she should've known their lives were about to change, but logic had told her to be skeptical of this obvious hustler.

"It chose you, each of you. Don't you even want to know why?"

Rose had tried to walk away. They all three had made the

attempt, but the gypsy had captivated their imaginations.

Each of them became increasingly enthralled and couldn't leave without knowing what the charismatic soothsayer predicted. When she finally had their full attention along with several dollars in her tip jar, she began her prophecies with the grand opening of *With a Twist*, the bar and bistro they'd been thinking of opening in San Diego's Gaslamp District. She predicted the business would bring them great success and wealth, which it had. She had even given them the details of the property's exact location and the date they'd be open for business.

The women hadn't thought much about those predictions at the time, but as the months clicked by and each prediction came true, their belief in the colorful gypsy had gone from doubt to complete certainty in her ability to see the future.

The gypsy had also predicted something more personal for each girl. Rose would hear from her estranged father and at long last they would cast aside their differences and begin to heal their wounded relationship.

The gypsy's words had brought up a well of emotion that Rose had thought she'd dealt with, but clearly she had not. She never could understand why her father had deserted her mom, and to hear a stranger talk about his return had been overwhelming.

The gypsy turned to them once again and gave a final warning. "Great things will come to you in the next twelve months. You will have success beyond your wildest dreams. But this heart is not a good luck charm. It is a symbol of love and you have been called by it. Each of you must fill up the heart and find your one true love. The trick is to have him willingly return your love before February fourteenth of next year, or everything you've gained will be lost."

With that last statement, Rose and her friends had walked away from the gypsy, lamenting over her dire warning, as if Valentine's Day had some special significance in the world of

177

magic. Still Rose couldn't shake the prediction about her father or about each of them finding their true love by Valentine's Day. And none of them could get over the warning about *losing everything* if one of them didn't "fill up the heart," whatever that meant.

Rose, with all of her logic, had brushed the predictions off as a fun event. Then when they opened *With a Twist* to great fanfare, she decided the gypsy had put the idea out there and they had simply followed through with it, getting the extra nudge they had needed to make their dream come true from the gypsy's prediction.

But when the red crystal heart turned up in Jasmine's office with no viable explanation for its presence, Rose began to believe in its power.

The gypsy's warning that all three *must* find love and have it returned or all three would lose everything wasn't exactly an encouraging prediction.

More like a calamitous threat!

Still, none of them had known the strength of the crystal heart until Jasmine had brought it into the bar area that very morning and placed it up on a shelf. She thought it was a nice touch for the upcoming romantic holiday. Rose, in her zest for cleanliness and sparkle, had taken it down momentarily to wipe off any trace of finger prints, and placed it directly in a small patch of sunlight that beamed through a skylight on the expansive walnut bar.

Now the heart radiated a brilliant unearthly red, a red so deep and so full of life it dazzled Rose as she stared across the bar at Max, who she hadn't seen in more than ten years.

This can't be happening, she thought as he finally noticed her staring at him, the red glow shining brighter with each step he took.

Rose hadn't officially opened the bar and bistro yet, but the front door had been unlocked for some deliveries. Max apparently had come in through that door, rolling a black carry-on suitcase behind him and a black backpack slung over one shoulder. He wore a black leather jacket, a black tight-fitting tee, and well worn jeans that hugged all the right places.

Maximilian Rosso had certainly grown tenfold into that childhood baritone voice he'd had, and was now walking toward her, with an aura around him that glowed a deep shade of sparkling red.

She wondered if his voice was still deep and sexy.

Of all the gin joints in all the world . . . Max just happened to be the one man Rose wanted more than air, but reason and past disappointments told her to keep her distance. She'd been down that rocky road with him before when they were teens and it had brought her nothing but grief and heartache.

Still, she had thought of him on more than one occasion, and whished with all her heart they would one day be lovers.

"Rosie?" he called out after a few seconds of checking her out, while a pulsating red sparkled all around him and dragged different shades of scarlet as he moved. It appeared as if all the degrees of color couldn't quite keep up with his movements, as if they were a moment out of sync with each other.

Could he see the glow?

She quickly moved the crystal out of the sunlight, but the darn thing wouldn't stop shining. She even covered it with a white bar towel. It had no impact. Instead, the crystal's beam grew more intense, as if it wanted to make sure she saw it.

"This place looks great." He gave her the once over. "You look great."

The raging glow seemed to have no impact on him. He just kept smiling, completely oblivious to what was happening all around him.

Rose wore a gray lose-fitting top that covered her hips, skinny jeans, and knee-high black boots. Not that she would keep the boots on once she began cooking, worn sneakers were good enough for that, but she liked to come into work looking decent. Now, as she stared at a glowing Max she wished she'd worn something that showed a little more of her curves and cleavage.

"Thanks," she mumbled. "So do you."

He looked more than great, incredibly sexy seemed like an apt description. Problem was, if his personality hadn't changed in the last ten years, his ego didn't need to hear anything more.

"That's my Rosie. Always quick with the compliments."

He dropped his backpack on the waxed wooden floor, stood his suitcase upright and walked behind the bar to give her one of those quick hugs a person would give to their aunt, or grandmother, the ruby red glow never leaving him.

"Where's that cousin of mine? She told me to meet her here." His voice echoed through the empty bar area, giving Rose a foreboding chill.

"In back," Rose told him, still trying to assimilate the crystal's obvious misguided exuberance.

Max resembled a Latin god with a face that could break a girls' heart with just one glance and a body guaranteed to bring her back for more.

"So, I hear you're a chef now." He took a step back and gave her another once over, smirking as his eyes traveled up and down her body. It gave her a rush of excitement. "Little Rosie Cupido, a chef. Who knew?"

"Just about everyone I ever came in contact with." Her excitement immediately changed to annoyance with his snide compliment.

He laughed, one of those deep baritone laughs that came from somewhere in his past. "I see you never lost your searing sense of humor."

"I see you never lost your ability to call me by the nickname I've always hated."

"Wow, I haven't seen you in ten years and you're still carrying a grudge?"

Rose crossed her arms under her chest. "Getting stood up for senior prom will do that to a girl."

He blew out a sigh. "I didn't stand you up, exactly. I sent you an email explaining why I couldn't make it."

"Who blows off prom night two hours before the dance with an email?"

"Rosie, I mean, Rose, I had no choice if I was ever going to meet and interview the Dalai Lama. I had to leave that night or I would have missed an incredible opportunity."

"As it was, you had the tour dates wrong, or so I heard, and he wasn't in LA that night. It was the next night. You could have double-checked the date before you went driving off, abandoning me for senior prom."

"Hindsight is always twenty-twenty."

"And a promise is a promise."

Just then Jasmine walked into the bar and squealed with delight at the sight of her ever traveling cousin. They hugged, a nice tight hug, one that Rose would have appreciated.

The red glow around Max diminished to a faint sparkle.

"When did you get in?" Jasmine asked.

"About an hour ago. This city has done some major changing since I've been home. And you." He quickly looked her over. "You, my fair cousin, look incredible. You're positively beautiful."

"Thanks," Jasmine said, soaking in the compliment. "So tell me everything. Your Facebook page has some major time gaps. I'm sure there's so much more to your travels. I want to hear all about where you've been, what you learned, who you've met, everything!"

They took seats at the bar, and Rose knew this was her time to bow out.

"Well, I've got a lot to do to prep for lunch. Nice to see you again, Max." Then she turned to Jasmine. "If you need anything, you know where to find me."

"Whatever you have to do can wait for an hour. Come on and sit down with us. I know you want to hear this as much as I do."

Jasmine had always played matchmaker with Max and Rose, but Rose was in no mood for it this morning. No way could she sit and listen to all the places he'd gone and everything he'd done without wishing she'd been with him. Of course, part of her knew she'd never have gone with him even if he had asked, which he most certainly did not. Still, the fantasy of their traveling together had lingered despite her logic.

"You two have a lot of catching up to do. I'm sure Max will be around for a few days. We'll talk later."

"Are you sure?" Jasmine coaxed, but Max seemed to have already forgotten that Rose was in the room. His full attention was on his favorite cousin.

Rose walked away certain the crystal had to be wrong. That it was simply wishful thinking on her part, there was no way rambling Max could ever love stick-in-the-mud Rosie. But when she turned back for one last look, the red glow surrounding Max was even brighter than ever.

Damn gypsy!

A Note from the Author

If you enjoyed this first chapter of **Stirring It Up**, we hope you will consider reading the complete book and exploring the rest of the series.

Remember to look for the other two books in the Love With A Twist series:

Book 1: Dirtying It Up by Calista Fox
Book 2: Shaking It Up by Erin Quinn

This novella was a treat to write because once again Calista Fox, Erin Quinn, and I have come together to bring you stories that intertwine. Writing with these two talented ladies is always a delight. This time, a bit of gypsy magic has captured the lives of three best friends who have opened a successful business together, and unless they can find true love by midnight on Valentine's Day, all their good fortune will be lost. A dire warning to be sure, but now that they've each met a man who can fulfill their dreams, the gypsy's prediction may not take hold. That is until things take a turn for the worse. Now, with each relationship being tested, and each love affair in jeopardy, there's nothing to hold them together but their friendship. Will the gypsy's warning come true or will Jasmine, Daisy and Rose be able to find true love before Valentine's Day come to a close?

Contact

You can find more of Mary's books listed on her Website:
www.maryleo.com

You can also find her on Facebook:
www.facebook.com/maryleoauthor

Follow her on Twitter @maryleoauthor

Other books by Mary Leo

Christmas With The Rancher
Aiming For The Cowboy
Falling For The Cowboy
The Spia Family Presses On
Her Favorite Cowboy
The Trouble With Bodies
Trusting Evil
Romancing Rudy Raindear
Stick Shift
A Pinch of Cool
For Better or Cursed

Afterword:

Thank you for reading our **Book Bites #1** and hope you have enjoyed this collaborative effort of fourteen authors from The Authors Billboard. We thank you for your support and hope we've provided you with a splendid array of work to choose from.

You can find most of these authors on the website at the Authors' Billboard.

If you enjoy Romantic Suspense, **Book Bites #2** has more selections of teasers for you to read.

Take care, stay well, and be kind to one another.

Bonnie Edwards

Donna Fasano

Traci Hall

Dani Haviland

Mary Leo

Dorothy McFalls

Nancy Radke

Mona Risk

Jacquie Rogers

Jennifer St. Giles

Alicia Street

Helen Scott Taylor

Katy Walters

Patrice Wilton

Latest info on free or reduced priced books at
www.authorsbillboard.com

Please follow us on Facebook:
www.facebook.com/authorsbillboard

www.ingramcontent.com/pod-product-compliance
Lightning Source LLC
Chambersburg PA
CBHW070916130626

46555CB00001B/159